# HOPE IN THE
# VALLEY

## ALSO BY MITALI PERKINS

Picture Books
*Between Us and Abuela*
*Home Is in Between*

Young Adult Novels
*You Bring the Distant Near*
*Forward Me Back to You*

# HOPE IN THE VALLEY

MITALI PERKINS

FARRAR STRAUS GIROUX
NEW YORK

*For my beautiful Ma —M.P.*

Farrar Straus Giroux Books for Young Readers
An imprint of Macmillan Publishing Group, LLC
120 Broadway, New York, NY 10271 • mackids.com

Our books may be purchased in bulk for promotional, educational,
or business use. Please contact your local bookseller or the Macmillan
Corporate and Premium Sales Department at (800) 221-7945 ext. 5442
or by email at MacmillanSpecialMarkets@macmillan.com.

Library of Congress Cataloging-in-Publication Data

Names: Perkins, Mitali, author.
Title: Hope in the valley / Mitali Perkins.
Description: First edition. | New York : Farrar Straus Giroux, 2023. |
Audience: Ages 8–12 | Audience: Grades 4–6 | Summary: Twelve-year-old
Indian-American Pandita Paul deals with change, grief, friendship, and
growing up in a community facing a housing crisis.
Identifiers: LCCN 2022046749 | ISBN 9780374388515 (hardcover)
Subjects: CYAC: East Indian Americans—Fiction. |
Self-actualization—Fiction. | Grief—Fiction. | Friendship—Fiction. |
Neighborhoods—Fiction. | LCGFT: Novels.
Classification: LCC PZ7.P4315 Hp 2023 | DDC [Fic]—dc23
LC record available at https://lccn.loc.gov/2022046749

First edition, 2023
Book design by Aurora Parlagreco
Printed in the United States of America by Lakeside Book Company,
Harrisonburg, Virginia

ISBN 978-0-374-38851-5 (hardcover)
1   3   5   7   9   10   8   6   4   2

THE BUTTERFLY COUNTS NOT MONTHS
BUT MOMENTS,
AND HAS TIME ENOUGH.

-RABINDRANATH TAGORE

# ONE

OUR FRONT PORCH IS A mess. Stepping around a discarded skateboard and a rusty tricycle, I avoid a couple of splintery wooden chairs and make my way down the steps. As I cross the street to the old Johnson place, I move slowly, casually, in case eyes are tracking me. The riskiest part of this escape is ducking behind the overgrown oleander bushes. But I'm careful as always.

There.

Now I'm hidden.

But I'm not inside yet.

Ma's makeshift wire twist still keeps the flap of fencing attached to its post. I unfasten it and the section swings slightly into the abandoned Johnson property like a gate, leaving just enough room for me to slip through. I came here almost every day last summer, and this summer, I plan to do the same. That's one advantage to living with three busy people—I can come and go without a lot of questions.

The first time I crawled through this opening, I was

four years old. I'd followed Ma across the street and into the prickly rosemary bushes. When she spotted me, she smiled, led me inside, and asked me to keep her escape a secret. Now I'm the only person on earth who knows how to get into Ashar Jaiga, as Ma and I called it. Ma's name, Asha, which means "hope," Ma's place, Ashar Jaiga. Place of Hope.

I need a dose of hope after my last conversation with Mr. Marvin. "Time steals your memories, Pandita," he told me. "These days I can't even recall the sound of my mother's voice." And then he'd sighed, a long, sad exhale that felt like it drew the breath out of me, too. "Work hard to remember, kid. I wish I had."

That's why I come here—to remember. I make my way between the oaks, pass an old water tank, and push through the tangle of weeds in what used to be straight rows of apricot trees. A few are starting to bear fruit. Every July, Ma and I tasted the ripe apricots that fell without getting bruised. We never took any home; they were ours to borrow, not to claim, Ma told me.

Roses, lilies, and lavender grow in the garden. The house didn't last as long as the garden and orchard, and what's left of it is rusted and broken. The front steps collapsed long before Ma started bringing me along, so I have to reach for the railing to pull myself up onto the sagging porch.

Here it is. My destination. A two-person porch swing—Ma's and mine.

I sink into one of the faded, flowery cushions. The glider still works and there's a spray can of oil nearby that I use if it starts to creak. I like it quiet—no sounds except for leaves rustling and birds singing. For a while, I sit there swinging. A dove hidden somewhere in the orchard sings a mournful tune. The melody reminds me of Ma singing.

She was quiet and so am I, but here, words poured out like the streams that water my grandparents' jute farm. Sitting side by side on this swing, she showed me how to weave garlands. Once our heads were crowned with flowers, she'd listen while I talked about school or shared my poems. Then I'd listen while she sang or told stories from the village where she'd grown up. Time seemed to stand still while I heard about close calls with crocodiles hidden along muddy banks, festival celebrations with cousins, rescuing chickens from a python that had crawled into the coop, and how she'd use rice powder paint to create alpana designs on the front step.

I pick up the cushion beside me and unbutton the cover. Hidden under the padding are my most precious possessions. First, four handwritten lavender-scented notes from Ma. They're short and I have them memorized, but I always open them anyway. I like to picture my mother's long, graceful fingers guiding a pen across the card, bangles clinking as she shaped the curves, dots, and lines of her penmanship. They're all addressed to *Dearest Pandu*, and each one is signed *Forever Yours, Ma*.

*When I long to be back in the village, being with you makes me feel at home again.*

*Your gift of words will bring joy and hope to the world.*

*Your quiet, listening spirit helps me share things I keep deep inside.*

*Reading so many good stories has made you courageous and loving.*

Rummaging again inside the cushion, I pull out a ribbon-tied stack of notes in my handwriting and a box of her scented stationery. Only two blank cards and matching envelopes are left now, one here and one in my room, and they're so old I can hardly smell any lavender. Ma used to buy them in bulk, but from where? I have no idea, and I can't ask Baba. There's nothing worse than seeing his jawline tighten at the sound of her name. Uncapping the pen I've brought along, I take one of the notecards and start writing.

*June 13, 1980. My darling Ma. It's my thirteenth birthday, so here I am. I met my goals from last year: to write one poem a month and read at least twenty-five books. This year, I can't think of any goal to set. All I really want is to go back in time, and that's impossible.*

*Anyway, Indy's cooking a special dinner and there's a pile of presents waiting. My best present, though, is that today was the last day of seventh grade. Now I get three blissful months before eighth grade. A whole summer without having to see Katrina Reed glued to Jemma's side, watching them pretend I don't exist.*

*Indy's probably wondering where I am, so I should get back. Ma, it's like I'm in a boat and you're on the shore and time takes us further apart with every birthday.*

*I miss you.*

*I love you.*

*Forever Yours,*
*Pandu.*

As I untie the ribbon and add this note to the others I've written, a twinge of worry over Mr. Marvin's words makes my stomach jump. *Are* my memories of Ma slipping away? The last birthday she celebrated with me was my tenth. All five of us were in India for some of that summer, but the days after June 23rd, 1977 are blurry in my mind. Mostly, I remember that we came back to California without her. Maybe that's why the last thing I've hidden inside this pillow is my favorite—a gift that my grandfather tucked into my hand before we left for the airport.

The black-and-white photo shows a girl standing in the shade of a banana tree. The handwriting on the back of the photo says, *Asha, age thirteen*, the age I am now. She's tall and lanky with no curves yet, like me. Her hair is in two braids—like mine—and she looks serious. But when I look closer, I see the stories and jokes in her eyes. I want to remember them forever, but how?

Time makes everything disappear—people, keepsakes, memories. *The Thief of Time*. Oooh. Good title for a poem. I'll have to write it later.

It swept the Johnsons away from this place.

My darling Ma will never visit Ashar Jaiga again.

Does it have to take my memories away, too?

I raise a fist against the sun, which is lower on the horizon now. I should at least put up a fight. If my enemy is going to turn me into a teenager today—whether I like it or not—I'm old enough to set a BIG goal. Let's call it . . . "Operation Remember Ma."

This means my sisters and I have to revoke the pact we made three years ago. It was Shar's idea, but Indy and I agreed to it right away. Baba looked so devastated every time Ma's name came up, we promised never to cry in front of him or talk about her at home. Now our silence has become a habit. A bad one, if you're trying to remember someone.

I'll call my mission ORM for short, because, as my English teacher says, what writer doesn't love a good acronym? ORM. ORM. Just repeating the letters in my head fills me with hope. Dropping a kiss on Ma's photo, I tuck it back into the cushion and head home.

# TWO

A BIRTHDAY CARD FROM INDIA is waiting in the mailbox. It's from our grandparents—the ones in the village, not the ones in the big city of Calcutta. We telephone Baba's parents once a week, but Didu and Dadu don't have a phone, so they send weekly letters. Holding it against my heart, I take off the canvas slip-ons I've worn since I was little. Every year I get a bigger size, but the style never changes. Just like the loose denim overalls and single-colored T-shirts I wear every day. Indy calls them my "uniform."

Leaving my shoes by the front door, I head to my room to open the letter in peace. I have to climb over heaps of laundry, washed and unwashed. We each do our own now; I'm the only one who uses a basket. The rest of the family uses the stairs. Every now and then Baba hires a cleaning lady but she doesn't tackle the laundry or the other STUFF that piles up everywhere. It feels like a beast that's growing, taking over every drawer and shelf and counter. Not my room, though—that's still nice and neat.

"That you, Pundit?" Indy calls from the kitchen. "Come get your birthday hug!"

I lean over the banister. "Coming! Ten minutes!"

Pundit. That's what my sisters call me. It means wise one. For some reason, they seem to think it fits. My other nickname is Pandu, but only my parents and grandparents call me that. To everyone else, I'm Pandita.

My room hasn't changed a bit since Ma sat in the wooden rocking chair by the window, reciting Emily Dickinson's poems or singing a Bangla lullaby until I fell asleep. The lemons in the tree outside still glow neon in the late-afternoon light. Ma stitched my patchwork quilt together from some of her old sarees and found me this writing desk with a locking drawer at a garage sale down the street. My pens and pencils are organized by color in jars arranged in neat rows, beside my poetry notebook and library books.

I use Ma's letter opener to slit the envelope and pull out the card. It has a picture of a rose on it. That's significant, because her parents used to call her "Gulgul," which means "little rose." Since Didu doesn't speak English and I can't read Bangla, Dadu writes for both of them.

*2nd June, 1980. Happiest of Birthdays, dearest Pandu! It's hard to believe you are turning thirteen. Thank you for sending another photograph with your last letter. These pictures are precious since we haven't seen you* in so long. The twins have become lovely young women, but you are looking more like your mother every year. We are glad to hear of your love of writing poetry. We would very much enjoy reading a poem of yours. We are devotees of the great Bengali poet Rabindranath Tagore, and the thought of having a poet in the family is thrilling.

Life in Bakkhali village continues. Your Didu is teaching three new music students how to play the harmonium. Monsoon rains flooded the river, muddying the lanes and jute fields, so I am working with town leaders to get more roads paved. One of the cows gave birth to a calf, which we hope you can assign a good name. We are keeping well. We pray for you three girls daily and long to see you. Please give your Baba our greetings. When are you coming to visit? Take all our love and blessings, Didu and Dadu

Reading their words makes me feel like I'm back on the balcony of their quiet house overlooking the pond and the jute fields. Almost, but not quite. They ask the same question at the end of every letter. *When are you coming to visit?* Three years of letters and I still don't have an answer. Well, maybe another step in ORM is to convince Baba that we need to go back to Bakkhali.

"PUUUUUN-DEEEEET!" Indy's practiced soprano soars up from the kitchen and reaches me through the closed door.

Grabbing our grandparents' letter, a pencil, and the last blank lavender-scented notecard in my drawer, I head to the kitchen, where my sister sweeps me into a hug.

"Happy birthday!" she says.

"Thanks." I lower my cheek to receive her kiss. "And thanks for cooking my birthday dinner, too. It smells great."

Indy whips out a lipstick from her apron front and starts re-applying it, handing me a tissue to erase the kiss mark. Her feathered hair is perfectly symmetrical on either side of her face, styled like almost all the girls in Sunny Creek. Including Jemma and Katrina. "I can't believe you're a *teenager*," she says. "AND three inches taller than Shar and me! How did *that* happen?"

"Must be your yummy cooking."

"I wish I could do it more often," she says. "I hate that we end up eating a lot of microwaved dinners."

"Or pizza. And cereal and grilled cheese. That's why it's so special when you cook. Want to read what Didu and Dadu have to say?" I hold out their card.

"Have to finish the eggplant," she says. "You read it to me."

I flip my braids out of the way and sit at the kitchen table. It's covered with bills, letters, the twins' home-work, and a pile of reports from Shar's job. The top one is titled, "Projected Housing Shortages in Silicon Valley: An Overview." Boring. I use my elbows to shove everything to the middle of the table, put my blank notecard and pencil in the cleared space, and read our grandparents' card aloud while Indy dips the eggplant in batter.

". . . . When are you coming to visit? Take all our love and blessings, Didu and Dadu." I emphasize the line about the visit just a little.

"Sounds like they're doing well," Indy says, pouring oil in the skillet and turning on the gas. "Tell them I miss them."

"Will do," I say. ORM, now or never. Then I add, "We need to ask Baba about visiting them again."

Immediately, Indy spins to face me. "Bad idea. You know he hates talking about the village. And what about the pact?"

I'd hoped Indy would be an easy ally. Tipping my head to one side, I flash the dimple in my left cheek and widen my eyes. "I'm glad you brought that up, Indy. It's my birthday, and the best present in the whole world would be . . . to end that pact. What do you think?"

She flinches as if the oil sizzling on the pan has hit her skin. "No. No way. Too soon. Besides, it was Shar's idea in the first place, remember? Good luck changing her mind." And with that, she turns back to the stove. The spatula starts flipping eggplant slices so fast it's flattening them into pancakes.

Guess I'll have to be as careful with words in this mission as I am when crafting a poem. Maybe truth is the way to go. "You two have four more years of memories than I do. And Baba has even more." I soften my voice. "I'm . . . afraid I'm starting to forget her, Indy. Will you at least be on my side when I bring it up with Shar?"

Sighing, my sister turns off the flame and transfers the squished eggplant to a plate. Now she's studying her perfectly applied red nail polish. When she finally looks up, her expression is . . . more thoughtful, I guess. Progress, right?

"It's sort of strange that you brought that up, Pundit. I've actually been thinking lately that Baba . . . well, it might be time for him to move on . . . by dating someone."

The back of my throat shuts down for a second. Indy hears the catch of my breath. "I had a hunch you'd hate the thought of that," she says. "But Baba's kind of handsome in an aging-Bollywood-actor kind of way, and I've caught a few ladies in town giving him the eye. What about a compromise? I'll back you up on revoking the pact IF you back *me* up about encouraging him to start dating."

And then, after scalding my heart, she moves to the sink and starts peeling a cucumber.

# THREE

I GLARE AT MY SISTER'S back. Dating? *Baba?*
No way. Never. I need him to *remember* Ma, not "move
on" with someone new. I calm myself down by starting
a reply to Didu and Dadu. After some thought, I choose
"Aloo" as the name of the baby bull, which means potato.
It's one of the few Bangla words I still remember.

*For my birthday feast, I asked for shinqharas with aloo
and pea, that yoqurty cucumber dip you call "raita," eggplant, and chicken curry with yellow rice. Indy's making
all of that right now, and it smells so, so good. She got
the hang of cooking from watching Ma. It's a good thing,
because the only appliance Baba, Shar, and I know how to
use in the kitchen—besides the fridge, of course—is the
microwave.*

I stop and erase the last sentence. This is why I always
write in pencil, so I can adjust words. Didu and Dadu

probably don't know what a microwave is. We only got ours a couple of years ago; I'm pretty sure they don't have those in Bakkhali. They don't even have electricity, if I remember right.

*I wish you could taste Indy's cooking, Didu and Dadu! Maybe one day you'll visit us and—*

Sighing, I flip my pencil and get rid of that sentence, too. Didu and Dadu can't afford plane tickets. Baba sends money to both sets of grandparents, and his parents use it to visit us every other year, but I think Didu and Dadu spend the money on food and medicine and stuff for the farm.

I hear the familiar sound of the garage door opening. A minute later, Baba comes in and deposits his briefcase on top of a tipsy stack of phone books and unread magazines. "What a day!" he says. It's his usual entry line. His spoken English has a trace of an Indian accent, but he's been here so long you can barely hear it. Ma's accent used to lilt up and down, like both sets of grandparents when they speak English. "Happy birthday, Pandu!"

His nickname for me sounds extra sweet today because Ma used it, too. I jump up to get one of his big hugs and catch a whiff of the computer science building at the university. He smells of musty textbooks, huge whirling machines, and blackboard chalk.

Baba lets go and I hold up the card from my grandparents in front of his face. "It's from Didu and Dadu. Want to read it?"

"Of course. Leave it right there on the table."

I square my shoulders. Indy's right—Baba avoids the word "Bakkhali" like it's a swear word, but today I have to say it. "It feels like yesterday when I turned ten. We celebrated that birthday in Bakkhali, remember?"

For a moment, he doesn't answer. Instead, he runs a hand through his thick, curly hair, and a shadow passes across his face. "I certainly do."

Indy gives me a "told you so" look but doesn't say anything.

"Where's your other sister?" Baba asks.

"Late, as usual," I say.

Baba frowns. "On your birthday? That's not good."

"Well, we can't wait, everything's ready," Indy says.

We move to the dining room, where Indy has cleared the round table by shifting junk to the corners of the room. She's set it beautifully with china plates, crystal glasses, a vase of orange roses, and tall, tapered candles. Indy's filled the glasses with orange juice to match the roses.

"Wow!" I say.

"So special and elegant!" adds Baba, carrying in the eggplant and shingharas.

I take my usual spot, trying not to focus on the empty

chairs. Ma's is still there between Indy's and Baba's. The five of us used to gather around this table almost every evening, but now we rarely eat in the dining room except for birthdays. The four of us don't even eat together too often in the kitchen. In a couple of years, Indy and Shar will leave for college. What's it going to feel like with just Baba and me at the table? My stomach clenches at the thought, even though I love being with him. If Asha means "hope" in Bangla, what's the opposite? Because sometimes this house feels full of that, whatever it is.

Indy puts the rice and chicken and the raita on the table and sits down. "I have news!" she says. "I've been trying not to spill it to Pundit because I wanted to tell you both at once. Shar already knows because she drove me to my interview. I got a job! You're looking at the newest salesclerk at Klegman's Department Store."

Well, there's a glimmer of hope. She's been job hunting for weeks. "Your favorite store!" I say.

"Congratulations!" Baba reaches across Ma's chair to squeeze Indy's hand. "Are they starting you at minimum wage? What is it now? Three dollars and thirty-five cents?"

"Nope. They're paying me a commission on everything I sell in the home goods section *and* in the young women's fashion section. I'm so happy—I'm going to make a ton of money selling things I love."

Baba pours raita on his biryani. "It's work, though, and that's always challenging. At least it is for me."

"Another hard day?" Indy asks.

"The new Computer Science department chair asked if I'd mentor a visiting faculty member from the Economics department! Why can't *they* take care of her? As if a full course load and my research wasn't enough! I'm so tired of—" He catches sight of my face. "But enough about work—time has flown by and it's your birthday again, Pandu."

Unfortunately, it is. Nothing I can do to stop my enemy.

"Before you say goodbye to being twelve, what were some good things that happened this year?" he asks. "I know seventh grade wasn't easy, and I'm proud of you for surviving it."

It's good to hear him say that. I thought nobody had noticed how hard it was to drag myself to school. "Well . . . I liked sharing library books with Mr. Marvin. And . . . some of the poems I wrote this year aren't *total* disasters. Number three is that Didu and Dadu were still around to write letters, and our other grandparents, too."

"That's a good list," Baba says.

Indy looks at the clock on the wall. "Time for cake."

"I'm a little worried about your sister," Baba says. "We'll have to call her office if she doesn't get here soon."

The cake's slathered with buttercream frosting, my favorite. Indy's decorated it with mango slices and shredded coconut to add her signature Indian touch. Baba and Indy start the happy birthday song, and I blow out the candles, trying not to think of Ma's sweet, lilting voice. This is one of those moments when I know all of us are missing her. Baba stops singing before the end, and when Indy has to carry the tune alone, her voice is off-key.

"What an amazing cake," is all I say when they're done.

Suddenly, the door bursts open and Shar rushes into the dining room. "So sorry, Pundit! Happy birthday!" After dropping a kiss on my cheek, she plops down in her usual spot. "Wait till you hear!" She pauses like a game show host about to announce a huge prize. "That property across the street is for sale!"

# FOUR

HAVE WE JUST HAD A massive earthquake? Is my chair shaking? I lean forward to see Shar's face. "Are you saying they're going to sell . . . the Johnson Orchard?"

"You got it, Pundit," she answers. "Our team was so excited we lost track of time. The Council has to approve demolition, but that's a done deal, we think."

*Demolition?*

But . . . that's *our* Place of Hope. Ma's and mine.

I can't breathe.

That's *our* porch.

That's *our* swing.

"And then what?" Indy's asking.

"Golden State Dwellings is going to try and buy the land," Shar says. "We want to build rental units over there."

"Get ready to face opposition," Baba says.

"Oh, definitely," Shar answers. "The Historical Preservation Society wants to keep the property as is, but that doesn't sound like preservation to me. It sounds like prejudice. We're gearing up for a fight."

The taste of biryani is rising in my throat. Swallowing hard, I manage to push it back down.

"Fight me, too," Indy says. "I don't want a bunch of strangers in our neighborhood."

"I agree," Baba says. "I like having a quiet orchard across the street."

Shar's in debate mode now. "That's the problem with this town! 'Not in MY backyard.' Saying *no* to rental properties is an old way of excluding people who don't have money. Sunny Creek only has two apartment buildings, and the units are too small for families with children. Some of our police officers, firefighters, nurses, and teachers can't afford to buy or even rent homes around here, and it's only going to get worse in the future. Where are *they* supposed to go?"

Where am *I* supposed to go? With a groan that must sound like I'm in agony, I drop my head in my arms to hide my face.

"Pandu, darling, what's wrong?" Baba asks immediately.

I don't answer. I can't. Confessing Ma's secret—*our* secret—feels like a betrayal. Besides, if I open my mouth, I might puke.

"Are you sick? Are you sad? What's happening?"

Then, as if he can't find more English words, he lets loose with some Bangla: "Ay, Bhagavan." *Oh, God*. It's his go-to phrase when he's overwhelmed.

My head feels like a boulder, but I lift it for his sake. Baba scans my face anxiously. The twins are telegraphing nonverbal messages to each other with eyebrows, chins, eyes, heads, and shoulders. I can't decipher their twin language like I usually do; Shar's words are barreling through my mind like bowling balls.

*For sale.*

*On the market.*

"Maybe I . . . I ate too much sugar," I manage to say.

"Well, then," Indy says brightly, "let's do presents!"

She brings over a department store bag that's obviously from her, a smaller gift bag, and a rectangular present. That must be from Shar, who always gives me books.

*Rental units.*

Swallowing hard, I tear off the paper from the book and read the title aloud: "*Take a Stand: A Primer for Young Activists*." Perfect for a younger version of Shar. "Thanks," I say. "Looks . . . interesting."

"You're welcome! Always trying to help you find your voice, little sister!"

*Demolition.*

I want to run to my room, but Indy's face looks so . . . hopeful as she pushes the large department store bag toward me. Inside, wrapped in tissue, is a flowery dress, perfect for a younger version of Indy. I force words out again: "Thanks, Indy. It's . . . so colorful."

"It's trendy but also kind of timeless so it reminded me of you," my sister says, smiling. "There's something else in the bag."

Digging through the tissue, I pull out a pair of high-heeled wedge sandals. The place where toes are supposed to go is narrow, pointy, and decorated with rhinestones. Horrible. There's no way I'm imprisoning my feet in these.

"Aren't they gorgeous?" Indy asks. "I thought the whole outfit might be perfect for an eighth grade dance."

There it is—eighth grade, looming at the end of the summer like a dark forest in one of Grimms' fairy-tales. How will I endure it without Ashar Jaiga? I won't. I can't.

"Open mine," Baba says, handing me the other gift bag.

Inside is a volume of poetry by Emily Dickinson. It's dog-eared and the cover is faded. I open the book and see a name in familiar handwriting: *Asha Paul*. My eyes sting. It's so, so good to hold a book that Ma loved in my hands.

"For the family poet," Baba says. "But keep going."

I reach back into the bag and take out a big box of the stationery Ma used to buy—fifty blank cards and fresh envelopes. I can't believe it—how did Baba know? I hug the box close and take in a deep whiff of lavender. Oh, Ma! They're going to tear down Ashar Jaiga!

I can't stay here another second, even though I don't want to ruin Indy's special dinner party. "I'm . . . Um, thanks, everyone. It's been a great birthday."

And after that massive lie, I run upstairs, lock my bedroom door, throw myself across the bed, and start life as a teenager by crying myself to sleep.

# FIVE

A ROAR OF MACHINERY OUTSIDE my window jolts me awake. I leap to my feet. It's morning. I'm still wearing my overalls and T-shirt from yesterday.

And then I remember: the demolition! I dash to the front door and hurl it open. Screeching to a halt on the porch, I gasp. What time did they start? How could they have done so much? Bulldozers and tractors are tearing down the old barbed wire enclosure, and our secret entrance is gone, along with the oleander bushes and the rosemary. Even the weeds are being ripped up in the claws of the bulldozers.

I try to see behind the machines to the house and the orchard. Looks like the fruit trees are still there. With the bushes and weeds gone, I can see the roof of the old Johnson house. It's still there, too.

For now, at least.

I have to get to our swing!

I race down the stairs and across the street. Baba shouts my name, but I don't stop.

One part of my brain registers the sharp asphalt under my bare feet. Before they hit dirt, a burly dude in a construction hat blocks my way.

"Stop, kid!" he yells. "You can't go in there! Where's your mother?"

Before I can answer, Baba's beside me. "I'm her father. Sorry, sir." He pulls me away from the man.

"Baba! I have to get in there!" I shout to be heard over the machines.

"Why?"

I move closer and he leans toward me: "I . . . I used to sneak through the fence sometimes." My confession is about one centimeter from his ear.

Baba's head jerks back. "What? But that's dangerous!" he yells. "I can't believe you did that!"

I tip his head back down so he can hear me. "Be mad at me later, Baba, but you've got to help before it's too late. I've hidden some . . . writing inside a pillow on the porch swing. Could you ask the workers to find it?"

He claps a hand to his forehead. "Ay, Bhagavan!"

But he goes over to the man who stopped me. They talk, and after raising a hand to pause the machines, the man disappears. Baba waits by the fence. I imagine big boots walking to the house, long strides covering ground faster than Ma's or mine. After what seems like forever, the man returns. My stomach sinks; he's shaking his head.

When they're done talking, Baba comes back. "Sorry,

Pandu, but there's no swing on the porch. The owner had everything moved off the property—furniture, books, papers—early this morning. I thought I saw a moving truck from my study window, but didn't pay much attention."

I swallow. Hard. "Are you sure? If I could go over there myself and look, maybe—"

"It's a demolition site now. It was dangerous before, and it's even more so now. Let's go home."

The roaring starts up again. Baba takes my hand and leads me back across the street. My heart is pounding along with the machines. The noise is not as loud in the front hall once the door is closed, but the bulldozers still sound like artillery.

Ma's handwritten letters.

My letters to her.

And that photo I loved so much.

Gone.

Indy comes down the stairs. "You okay, Pundit?" she asks.

I don't answer; I can't. My heart feels like someone's bulldozing inside my chest, and worst of all, I'm breaking our sister pact by crying in front of Baba. He pulls me into his arms and holds me close, just like he did that day three years ago in the village. The day Ma didn't come home from the hospital. Indy's hand is patting my back.

"Please stop, Pandu, please," Baba says after a while, and his voice is unsteady.

Indy gives my shoulder a little squeeze.

It's a reminder.

I force myself to swallow the next sob. And the next. After a minute or two, I pull out of Baba's embrace and wipe my cheeks with the sleeve of my pajama top.

"I'll be okay," I mutter.

Then I turn and trudge up the stairs, leaving Indy and Baba in the entry. I collapse on my bed, letting the tears flow freely now that I'm alone. The bulldozer's roaring inside my brain now. Ma's letters. I'll never be able to study her handwriting, open the envelopes, pretend I'm reading her words for the first time.

At least I still remember the beautiful words she wrote. For now, anyway. Jumping up, I grab my composition book and scribble the lines I've read so often they're grooved into my brain, like the lyrics to favorite songs.

*When I long to be back in the village, being with you makes me feel at home again.*

*Your gift of words will bring joy and hope to the world.*

*Your quiet, listening spirit helps me share things I keep deep inside.*

*Reading so many good stories has made you courageous and loving.*

They're not in her handwriting, but at least now I'll never forget the words. I wish I could do the same with my letters to her, full of confessions and struggles from the past three years. Those are probably incinerated by now. And that precious photo. Dumped in a landfill somewhere? Or burned, too?

We have other photos, pushed back now behind the clutter in this house, but they were taken after she married Baba and became our mother. Studying that one of her as a girl in Bakkhali always felt like reading a preface, or a prequel, to a story I love.

Suddenly, the roar of machinery stops again.

Through my open window, I hear someone shouting. "Don't you dare touch that house!"

It's a woman's voice.

Loud.

Strong.

And *very* familiar.

# SIX

I RACE DOWNSTAIRS AGAIN AND peer out the front door. It *is* my friend Ms. Maryann, the town librarian, just as I'd thought. She's wearing a forest green tracksuit with stripes that match her white tennis shoes. She and a semicircle of three other women are confronting the worker who stopped me earlier. He's holding up his palms like a shield and trying to back away, but they've got him surrounded. I can hear his defense from our house.

"Okay, ladies, we're not going to demo the house. At least not today. Or the trees, I promise. The city has to issue a permit for that. We're just clearing the perimeter and putting up a new security fence."

"I'm glad, young man," says Ms. Maryann. "Because *we*—the members of Sunny Creek Historical Preservation Society—will be saving the house, the cottages, and that beautiful old orchard. The entire property is a treasure! It's going to be our next town park and museum. History matters, even if the person who hired you doesn't give a fig. Or an apricot, for that matter."

I can hardly believe what I'm hearing. Ashar Jaiga—a park and museum? And then I remember Shar had said something about the Society yesterday, but I hadn't registered it.

"Listen, lady. I'm just the site foreman. I have no idea who's paying for this project. I'm only doing my job—putting up a security fence."

Turning away, the women talk among themselves. I put on my shoes and head down the porch steps to the sidewalk. One of Ms. Maryann's companions is a tall, thin woman with silvery, short hair. She's wearing a pinstripe pantsuit with padded shoulders. After a bit, she plants fists on hips and speaks in a loud, confident voice to her companions.

"Well, they won't be able to keep it secret for long. We've called a special Council meeting this Saturday to see whether this property can be preserved. So, the people who own this place will have to show up and face us."

I hear Ms. Maryann sigh. "I hope you're right, Bev. Anyone who owns a chunk of Sunny Creek land these days can pay lawyers to handle the whole shebang."

"Well, they're not bulldozing that house," says Ms. Pinstripe. "Not today."

"Not ever," another woman retorts. She's in a purple tracksuit with bleached blond hair that looks like a sculpture made of hairspray.

With that, the four of them—pinstripes-with-shoulder-pads, my friend Ms. Maryann, tracksuit lady, and a petite redhead with a cane—start marching back and forth in front of the silenced machines and watching workers. They're chanting, "Not today. Not EVER! Not today, NOT EVER!" A few neighbors come out to see what the commotion is about.

Ms. Maryann spots me and beckons. "Join us, Pandita!"

I hesitate. What can chanting do? If Ms. Maryann and her friends lose, the whole place will get torn down. And if they win, I won't have Ashar Jaiga to myself anymore. But at least I'll get to visit. The house will stay standing. That front porch might still be there.

I cross the street and add my body to the line of middle-aged marchers.

Ms. Maryann grins at me as my voice joins the chant: "Not today! Not EVER!" I may not be loud, but I mean every word.

After a while, the four of them stop to catch their breath so I do the same.

"Friends, we'll meet Monday evening at Margaret's house to plan our strategy," says Ms. Maryann. Then she turns to me. "Pandita, you'll join us, I hope? Remember what the poet George Santayana said: 'Those who cannot remember the past are condemned to repeat it.'"

I look around at the semicircle of wrinkled faces. This army of history lovers might be my last hope when it comes to ORM. "I'll have to ask my father first," I say. "But if he says yes, I'm in!"

I peek through the half-open door before walking into Baba's small study. Indy and Shar are in there, too. My sisters are dressed for school; high school still has one more week before summer vacation. Indy's in three-inch wedge heels and lipstick that matches her red dress, which is as short as she can wear without Baba starting to scold. Meanwhile, Shar's wearing her debate team power outfit: tweed fitted blazer with white shirt, black pants, and black flat saddle shoes. She keeps her hair cropped short and spurns makeup.

I'm glad Shar's not anywhere near the window because I'd hate to think of her spotting me marching with the Society. The longer Shar doesn't know about my alliance, the better. I'm not looking forward to defending myself when she starts arguing.

I push the door open all the way. "Hello, family!" I say, trying to make my voice sound normal.

All three of them jump.

"Pundit! You came in so . . . suddenly. Did you hear—"

Shar's sharp elbow makes Indy stop talking. "I was just telling Baba about a great way to keep you busy this summer."

They were probably discussing my two out-of-control episodes in the last twenty-four hours. I'll admit, it's not normal behavior for me. "I don't like being busy," I say.

"Here, look at this," Shar says, holding out a color-ful brochure. "It's the catalog of summer recreation pro-grams in Sunny Creek. I'm thinking . . . why don't you try the drama camp Indy loved so much?"

I don't take the catalog. "Drama's Indy's thing, not mine. Can you guys clear out? I need to talk to Baba about something."

After a second or two, Shar drops the catalog on Baba's desk. But the star debater of Sunny Creek High School doesn't give up that easily. "The camp's at your school—you can walk from here," she says. "Ms. Harper also coaches the debate team. Her lessons in enunciation and diction helped me so much. This is a perfect chance to gain some confidence about speaking up."

Gritting my teeth so hard my jaw hurts, I throw Indy a pleading look to intervene.

She throws one right back at me. "You're actually really good at singing, Pundit, you've just never tried it in public. Plus, Lily's volunteering as an intern this sum-mer. You love Lily."

Okay, Lily's amazing. But still! You, too, Indy? "I told you, drama's not my thing. Could I *please* talk to Baba alone?"

Baba puts a hand on each of my sisters' backs and

ushers them to the door. "Okay, you two, I'm the parent here, remember?"

As soon as the door is shut, I blurt out my question: "Baba, can you drive me to a meeting of the Sunny Creek Historical Society on Monday night?"

He spins out his swivel chair for me and perches on the edge of his desk. "Tell me more, Pandu."

Once he hears that the Society is going to be fighting Shar's nonprofit's plan to buy the property, he gives me a searching look. "Sounds like we're heading into a Paul family civil war."

"Maybe. But I'll find out more at the Society meeting."

"Who else will be there?"

When I tell him the members of the Society are my favorite children's librarian and three other middle-aged ladies, he puts down the brochure. "It sounds okay, Pandu, but . . . I'll make you a deal."

My heart sinks. Why is my family so into bargaining? First Indy, now Baba.

"You can join this Historical Society on one condition." He takes a big breath. "That you . . . also enroll in that summer drama camp your sisters were talking about."

I jump to my feet. "WHAT? Baba, no! WHY?!"

"Shar and Indy both think it might help you make some friends your age, and I have a feeling they're right."

"They're always trying to 'help' me, but I don't need it!"

Baba just looks at me, picks up the catalog, and starts leafing through it.

I switch tactics. "Isn't there a writing camp I could join instead? Or a poetry camp?"

Baba shakes his head as he keeps flipping pages. "Swimming, tennis, basketball . . . unfortunately, there's nothing for junior high students in the arts except drama. Besides, you can't just stick to the familiar, Pandu. It's good to try new things." He sighs, as if he knows what he's about to say isn't going to make me happy. "Drama camp, or no Historical Society."

"But I have to . . ." I can't explain why I so desperately want to save the Johnson property.

"To what, Pandu?"

I don't answer. I can't. I move to the window instead. Outside, a high fence is going up so fast, it looks like we'll be living across the street from a prison by dinnertime.

Baba walks over and puts his hands on my shoulders. Gently, he turns me, palms my cheeks, and looks right into my eyes. "I know I'm not doing this parenting job very well on my own, but won't you give this drama camp a try, Pandu? For me?"

Dang it. It's almost impossible to say no when he asks like that. "Ugh. Okay."

"Thank you, darling. Camp starts Monday at ten. It's over by three and it only lasts four weeks. You can handle that, don't you think?"

# SEVEN

I WAKE UP EARLY WITH my jaw aching. Must have clenched it all night. I dreamed of apricot trees getting bulldozed and the twins pushing me onstage while a bunch of kids from school laughed in the audience. I can't believe I was sad about my sisters leaving for college. Thanks to them, my quiet, unhurried summer is becoming a war zone of stress. First, the threatened destruction of Ashar Jaiga. Next, the loss of my precious possessions. Now—*drama camp*?!? I sure hope Jemma and Katrina aren't signing up. That would definitely be the stuff of nightmares.

Massaging my jaw, I head outside and stop for a minute to scowl at the new fence across the street. A sign is posted on it. NO TRESPASSING. PRIVATE PROPERTY. The tight mesh reaches up from the ground to about double my height. Those angry-looking loops of needled wire across the top would slice anyone who tried to climb over.

I walk on. I can't wait to tell my bad news to Mr. Marvin. He's sure to understand. The June day is trying to cheer me up with perfect weather: fresh air; sunshine; a light breeze; roses, daisies, and geraniums in every garden. Close to the center of Sunny Creek, on the same street as the junior high school, library, and Town Hall, is Orchard Manor, the senior care facility owned by the mother of my ex–best friend.

When Mrs. Kim called last fall to ask if I wanted to volunteer as a library aide, I didn't say yes right away. But then I thought: Why not? It won't kill me to bring a few books to an old person and maybe, just maybe, I'll run into Jemma. *Without* Katrina attached. So, Baba signed permission forms, and I got assigned to Mr. Marvin. Sadly, I didn't see Jemma when I visited, but at least I made a new friend.

"Your book partner doesn't like talking much," Mrs. Kim warned during my training session.

"Neither do I," I answered, making her smile.

At first, I visited only on Saturday mornings. I'd pick up a book to return, head to the library, and then swing by again to drop off my next selection. It took a while to win Mr. Marvin over. I noticed that he clammed up around chatty nurses and aides, so I didn't say a lot. After a while, we started discussing books I was bringing. He liked my choices, I could tell. I've even started sharing my poems with him—once I've honed and polished them, that is. Reading them to him usually leads to tweaking a word or two that makes them even better.

Oh, good, there he is, on the porch. He waves as I get closer. Orchard Manor used to be blocky and boring, but Mrs. Kim remodeled it last year. Now the house looks like a mansion, with rocking chairs on a spacious front porch, white columns, and roses in bloom. Old people are lured here with the promise of gourmet food, lectures from top professors, spa treatments, and concierges who plan everything from five-star travel experiences to health care. All of which stink, according to Mr. Marvin. He's one of the "idiots who fell for the sales pitch," as he puts it.

I climb the stairs to sit in the rocking chair beside him.

"Hey, kid," he says. "I'd offer you some of this sorry excuse for tea but it's too sweet and lukewarm. This place! Underwhelming and overpriced. Like everything in California. Why I left Minnesota, I'll never know."

"Remember the snow, Mr. Marvin."

"You got a point there—no more shoveling. And that Mrs. Kim person hired a new head nurse who seems . . . good. I like her."

I almost fall off my rocker. Mr. Marvin, saying something positive about a staff member at Orchard Manor? This nurse must be an angel in disguise . . . no, the superhero of nurses. Yes, that's better. "Hmmmm," I say.

He settles back into his chair. "You promised me a poem, right? I've been counting the days to hear it."

I *had* promised, but my heart feels too raw for criticism.

Slowly, I pull out my poetry notebook. "No feedback, Mr. Marvin. You can give it to me another time. Please."

"Got it." He closes his eyes as I start reading.

*It's raining in the forest*
*The wind is fresh and free*
*Squirrels running here and there*
*Trees bending in wild glee*
*The birds are so excited*
*And gladness fills the air*
*The brook turns to a fury*
*But no one seems to care*
*Sweet-smelling rain caresses*
*The flowers and the plants*
*And all the forest sways in tune*
*To the wind's inviting dance*

When I'm done, Mr. Marvin takes in a big inhale, and then another.

"Why are you breathing so loudly?" I ask.

"Smelling the rain," he says.

I can't help smiling for the first time since Shar broke the news about the Johnson place. Sunny Creek hasn't had rain in months. It's high praise.

We sit and rock for a while, and then he throws me a look. "So, you're a teenager now, eh? Happy belated."

He remembered. That's what friends do. "Yep," I say.

"That's getting up there. For some reason I can't imagine you turning into a grown-up."

"I can't, either. And I don't want to."

"Well, unhappy belated, then. Is that why you look so glum?"

"I got bad news on my birthday, Mr. Marvin."

"Oh dear," he says, sitting up.

"They're demolishing the property across the street. That beautiful old orchard and house! Can you believe it? *And* Baba's making me go to drama camp this summer. Drama camp! Me!"

He's quiet. And then: "That's rough, kid. Not much you can do about the property, so I'd let that one go. But drama camp sounds dreadful. I'm sorry."

His sympathy is making me feel better. I knew it would. "Some birthday, huh?"

"They're always a downer for me," he says. "But hold on, I have something to give you. Wait here."

He leans on the arms of the chair to hoist himself up, and I prop one foot underneath the runner to steady it. Mr. Marvin's so small I hardly feel any weight on my shoe. His skin looks like crinkly white cloth draped around a bony sculpture. After he disappears through the screen door, I wait and rock, inhaling the smell of roses wafting up from the garden.

When Mr. Marvin returns, he's carrying a library book and an old straw hat trimmed with blue ribbon.

"For your birthday," he says, handing me the hat. "It was my mother's. I had it cleaned, and they replaced the ribbon."

The hat feels light and airy on top of my braids. "A farmer's hat," I say. "Matches my overalls. I love it."

"You remind me of Garnet in *Thimble Summer*."

"So, you liked the book?" I asked.

"Absolutely. You know, when I was a kid, I used to read books like Tom Sawyer or the Hardy Boys. Adventures, boy heroes. I enjoyed them, mind you, but I missed out. Until you came along." He glances around and lowers his voice to a whisper. "Now I absolutely love reading stories with girls in them."

I'm sure the staff and residents of Orchard Manor never see this side of Mr. Marvin. Around them, he grunts and complains a lot. "I'm bringing you *The Betsy-Tacy Treasury* by Maud Hart Lovelace next—it's set in Minnesota. You'll love her descriptions of the seasons."

"Get going then," he says. "I'll be waiting for it after my nap."

I put *Thimble Summer* in my bag and jump up from the rocking chair, almost losing the hat. Steadying it on my head, I skip down the stairs.

"Thanks for the present, Mr. Marvin! I love it."

The ancient hat seems to fill my head with hope. Maybe I'll make it through drama camp without any drama. Ms. Maryann and the Society will save the house and orchard, I'm sure of it. And, somehow, I'll convince my sisters to revoke that pact.

But then I see her: Jemma Kim, my ex–best friend, sitting on a bench in the courtyard in front of Town Hall.

She's with Katrina Reed.

As usual.

# EIGHT

I WHIP OFF THE HAT. Why'd I do that? As if I care what they think about my clothes. But I duck behind a nearby tree anyway, trying to hide both myself and the hat.

What *they're* wearing is right on trend, according to Indy—high-waisted cut-offs, tube tops, and wedge sandals like the ones I got for my birthday, which make their feet look like they're perching on pieces of pie. Jemma's black hair is styled exactly like my sister's, as if a curling iron can magically turn a Korean thirteen-year-old into that blond actress every girl in Sunny Creek seems to be imitating.

I have to admit, though, that Katrina *does* look a little like that actress. Along with being blond, she's blue-eyed, tall, curvy (already!), and stands with her shoulders back and head up. Her family has lived here for generations and has a boatload of money. Plus, a literal boat. Only a chosen few from Sunny Creek Junior High have been invited to cruise the Bay in the Reed boat. Jemma probably goes all the time. Why did Miss Sunny Creek have to pick *my* best friend to become *her* best friend? She could have anyone she wanted.

Katrina has a portable cassette player on her lap, and she and Jemma are singing along to a Blondie song at the top of their lungs: "COVER ME WITH KISSES, BABY, COVER ME WITH LOVE . . ." Their voices are so *loud*. Does the entire town have to listen to them sing? I know the song, too, but you won't catch *me* singing in public. I can't help noticing, though, that Jemma sounds good. Really good. That's not surprising; she's been part of her church's children's choir for years.

Katrina switches off the player. "Yuck! I sound terrible. *You* sound great, though."

"Play it again?" Jemma asks. "Maybe I'll use that song for my audition."

"You can't use a popular song," Katrina says. "We'll have to sing a song from whichever musical the teachers pick."

*Audition? Musical?* That sounds like drama camp! I stifle a groan. I'm about to sneak away to the library when Katrina spots me hiding. She whispers something into Jemma's ear, and the two of them laugh. Now it feels like I'm inside my own nightmare. The whole situation's stuck in the toilet. Wish I could flush it.

"Hey," I say, stepping into full view.

"Hey," Jemma replies.

"Hey," echoes Katrina.

As I trudge up the library stairs, one of Dickinson's poems pops into my head. It's called "Friends," and Ma recited it so often at bedtime that I have it memorized.

*Are friends delight or pain?*
*Could bounty but remain*
*Riches were good.*
*But if they only stay*
*Bolder to fly away,*
*Riches are sad.*

That's right. If only my friendship with Jemma had remained instead of flying away.

Seeing Ms. Maryann makes me feel better. She hands me a bag of freshly baked chocolate chip cookies for my birthday, tells me how glad she is that I'm joining the Preservation Society's battle to save the Johnson property, and helps me find *The Betsy-Tacy Treasury* for Mr. Marvin.

Thankfully, as I walk back to Orchard Manor munching a cookie, the Blondie duet isn't in sight. Mr. Marvin isn't out on the porch, either, so I knock.

A petite woman in a nurse's uniform opens the door. Her name tag says, ALODIA CORPUZ, NURSING MANAGER. Oh! This must be the super nurse that made Mr. Marvin miraculously like her. I scan her face, which is about the same shade as mine. She's not Indian, is she? Her name doesn't sound like it.

Her smile puts me at ease, so I gather my courage to speak up. "Is Mr. Marvin up from his nap? I'm his library aide."

"Welcome!" She does have a knockout smile. "You must be Pandita the Poet; Mr. Marvin told me about you. What a sweetie you are to visit him. I'm sad to tell you he wasn't feeling too well after he woke up, but I'll let him know you came by."

"What happened, er"—I read her name tag once more—"Nurse Corpuz? Did he fall again?"

"No, no, nothing like that. He's a bit low, that's all. Growing old is hard enough, and then when you don't have family around . . . Don't worry, the cook put cornbread muffins in the oven, and I'll take some up to him."

"Oh . . . well, please tell him I stopped by. Here's his book. And Mr. Marvin loves 'a bite of muffin with a bowl of butter.'"

She chuckles as she takes *The Betsy-Tacy Treasury*. "And 'a few crumbs of scone with a tub of clotted cream.' I've already heard that one."

"Thanks." I turn to go.

The nurse calls after me. "Pandita, wait! Aren't you a student at Sunny Creek Junior High?"

Slowly, I rotate again. "Er . . . yes. I'll be in eighth grade in September."

"Oh, that's wonderful! Our son, Leo, will be starting there as an eighth grader, too. He doesn't know a soul around here, and that's always hard. I'm so glad he'll be able to meet you!"

*Me? The social outcast of Sunny Creek Junior High?* My feet start shuffling backward. I manage to return her smile before launching myself in the direction of home.

# NINE

ON MONDAY MORNING, WHEN I come downstairs, my stomach is doing flips like the pancakes Indy's cooking on the griddle.

Shar pats the stool next to her. "We're driving you to drama camp, Pundit."

"No, thanks," I say, keeping my tone frosty. But I sit down. Those pancakes smell *amazing*.

"We know you're mad," Indy says, stacking pancakes on a plate and handing it to me. "Sorry that we love you so much."

Shar passes me the syrup. "Baba suggested we drive you and help you enroll. He filled out forms and left a check, so let us do this, okay?"

"I can handle it," I say. But I'm thawing, I can tell. It's so nice to have them both home in the morning for once. My stomach is settling down. I pick up my fork and take a big bite of perfect pancake.

"We know that, but we want to go with you," Indy says, sitting down to join us. "Please, Pundit?"

I shrug. "You can drop me off. But you're *not* coming in."

My sisters are messaging nonverbally, but I ignore their twinnishness and finish off my pancakes.

"You sure you want to wear those overalls?" Indy asks after a bit. "All the other girls will—"

"INDY! I don't care what everyone else is wearing. I like my overalls."

"Okay, okay," Indy says, serving me another stack. "Besides, after today, Ms. Harper will have everyone wearing the same thing."

I don't ask for details. "Well, I'm going to keep wearing overalls until they come back in style. And can you two *please* stop managing my life?"

Shar takes the syrup bottle and drowns her pancakes. "We do get kind of bossy, don't we?"

"Finally, the truth," I say, but I can't help smiling. Shar in humble mode? Unusual. Maybe this is a good time to press forward with ORM. But how?

"I'm so glad other people are going to enjoy your beautiful voice," Indy says.

Perfect. Thanks, Indy. Here we go. "Ma was a good singer," I say. "I can't remember the Bangla words to the songs she sang, but I know her voice was sweet."

Shar's face reminds me of the NO TRESPASSING signs pasted on that fence across the street. But Indy looks over at me, takes in a big breath, and says: "She *was* good, Pundit. Her voice sounded a lot like yours, in fact."

I *knew* she'd come through. "It did? How I wish I could hear it again!" And then I gather more courage. "I'd . . . I'd really like to talk about Ma more. It's been three years . . . What do you guys think about putting an end to the pact?"

Dead silence. I nudge Indy's shin with my foot.

"I think . . . well, maybe it *is* time," she says. "Baba seems like he's ready to move on. Even maybe . . . to meet someone new?"

It's her big toe's turn to poke my ankle, but I can't bring myself to accept her terms of the deal. My ankle gets poked again, but still I don't say anything.

Shar's scowling at her plate as if it's the one breaking our sister pact. "Baba doesn't seem ready to me. *At all.* For any of that."

I steer a piece of pancake around the pool of syrup with my fork. "What about if we share memories when he's not around?"

But even as I make the suggestion, my heart sinks. Moments like this aren't that common. I can't remember the last time the three of us sat down to breakfast together.

"Let's talk about it later," Shar says. "You've got a big day ahead, Pundit. You need to focus."

Well, at least she didn't say no. I reach for the butter dish and lop off a yellow rectangle for what's left of my pancakes.

When Indy and Shar drop me off at the curb, kids that I thought I wouldn't have to see until September are walking with their mothers into the building.

Shar hands me the form signed by Baba and a check. "Channel your Bengali power, Pundit."

"Will do," I say.

Shar always says knowing our specific culture is a gift. Almost everyone in Sunny Creek is white except us, a few other Asian families, and a couple of Black teachers at the high school. We're the only Indian family here.

"I made your lunch today, but after this, you're on your own," Indy says. "I'll be busy making money!"

I grab the sack lunch she's dangling out the window. "Thanks."

They drive off. The pancakes are trampolining inside me now. After finding the registration table, I slip into the back of the line. Ahead of me is Jemma. With her, glancing impatiently at her watch, are Mrs. Kim, Katrina (of course), and Mrs. Reed. Both moms are wearing crisply ironed blouses, tight skirts, and high heels, but they aren't talking to each other.

My mother and Mrs. Kim used to be friends.

Everyone but me seems to have a mother along.

Maybe I should have let my sisters walk me in. Or asked Baba to come.

I remember standing so close to Ma that the silk of her saree brushed against my skin.

I remember how it felt.

I remember how she smelled.

A familiar, terrible wave rises inside me.

Back when they used to drown me, coming so fast one after another that I could barely breathe, Ms. Maryann gave me a way to survive. She learned it after she lost her husband to cancer.

You breathe in and out.

You wait.

You tell yourself: The tide will go out. The waves will recede.

And repeat.

They'll start to slow.

But oh, how each one crashes as it lands.

The line in front of me moves forward.

Bit by bit, the waves stop coming.

After a while, I'm able to look around again. Mrs. Kim waves at me as she hurries out of the building. For a second, Jemma's eyes meet mine, but she looks away before I get my face muscles to cooperate. Oh, how I wish we could be friends again!

Well, if I have to be at drama camp with her all month, why not add another goal to my birthday list? I could launch Operation Win Back Jemma, too. This could be the summer of ORM *and* OWBJ.

And the first step in OWBJ?

Give my ex–best friend one smile that she receives.

Just one.

Stepping forward in line again, I turn a corner and spot Nurse Corpuz from Orchard Manor. She's with a kid my age, probably her son that she wants me to meet. He's carrying a guitar, wearing jeans and a white T-shirt, and his hair is long and curly. What's he trying to look like, a rock star? The strange thing is that he *does* kind of look like a celebrity. None of the boys in my grade wear their hair like that, long and loose. He stands out, but it doesn't look strange. Girls around me start giggling and whispering; they can't keep their eyes off him. He's, well, *eye-catching*. Why would someone like *that* need help making friends from *me*?

Suddenly, he turns and sees me staring. I drop the form and bend to get it. When I come back up, Nurse Corpuz is in front of me, and so is her son.

"Pandita! I'm so happy you're joining this camp, too! Leo, this is Pandita, the girl I was telling you about."

He grins, and I see braces on his teeth. Okay, so he isn't perfect. Not yet, anyway. Somehow, that makes me feel better.

"Nice to meet you," I say, and he smiles again.

My cheeks are warm. Usually, I avoid talking to boys, and they do the same with me, but this one is still looking at me. Probably wondering where my mom is. That's the problem with kids who weren't in Sunny Creek Elementary back in fifth grade when the news about Ma landed and everyone got uncomfortable around me.

# TEN

THE MOTHERS FINALLY LEAVE. AND we're herded into the school auditorium. As Leo follows me to the back row, Katrina turns to stare at us. At Leo, really. And she's not the only one. A new kid always attracts attention, but this one has dimples, golden-brown skin, curly, shiny hair, and an aura of confidence that's magnetic. They're probably wondering why he's sitting next to me, of all people. I'm wondering the same thing.

I count twenty-nine Leo-ogling heads that belong to seventh graders. Rising eighth graders, I mean. Jemma makes thirty, but she's keeping her eyes on the stage. The only person in the room paying attention to me is . . . Leo.

He flashes a smile that looks exactly like his mother's. "Why are they all staring? Do I have food in my braces?"

I glance at his mouth and look away quickly. "No. No food. It's just that . . . well, you're new. The rest of us have been together since preschool."

Near the front I spot two friends of Indy's who've been performing with her in musicals for years. Lily's a petite redhead with freckles and a big smile, and Tom's movie-star handsome, with shoulder-length brown hair and a deep singing voice. Indy and Lily talk about him as "Handsome Tom" behind his back, so I call him that in my head. Lily catches my eye and waves, and I give a little wave back.

"Who's that?" Leo asks. "She looks like she's in high school."

"My sister's friend. They're in theater together." And then, for some reason, I can't help bragging: "My sister gets most of the leads, though."

"And who's the David Cassidy look-alike?"

Handsome Tom *does* look like the pop star Indy has a crush on. Hmmmm. I'll have to ask her about that. "That's Tom. He must be an intern, too."

Ms. Harper, Mr. Jackson, and the two interns climb the stairs to the stage. Ms. Harper is tall and made of sharp angles—elbows, knees, jaw, forehead. The only round things on her body are dozens of silver bangles that line each of her wrists. Her hair is silvery, too, but the skin on her chiseled face is smooth. She looks even more pale, tall, and thin next to short, chubby Mr. Jackson, who has a medium-sized afro and is wearing a plaid suit and a bow tie.

"Welcome, campers," Ms. Harper says. "We're going to be producing a special musical this summer. Mr. Jackson, why don't you tell them what we've chosen?"

"You'll be performing in one of the classic musicals of the century!" Mr. Jackson says, beaming. "*The Sound of Music!*"

Immediately, the whole theater is buzzing with excitement. Honeybees are inside me, too, because that's one of my absolute favorites. I love the story of a young woman named Maria who leaves a convent to become a governess and brings music and romance to a rich Austrian widower with seven children. Lily's grinning at me from the stage. I've sung all the songs with her and Indy. And Jemma, too, back when we used to have sleepovers. As if on cue, her head turns for a second and our eyes meet, but she immediately swivels it again.

"I've seen that movie at least five times," Leo says. "This is great."

"Seven for me," I answer, surprising myself again. Pandita Paul, oversharing? Weird.

Ms. Harper claps her hands to get our attention, making her bangles clink like the church bells in the opening scene of *The Sound of Music*.

"Settle down, settle down. I like hearing your voices, though. Do you know that no people on earth since the beginning of human history have ever shared the same voiceprint? Your voice is as unique to you as your fingerprints."

She pauses, letting that sink in. It *is* amazing, especially given the number of people who live or used to live on the planet. This morning Indy told me that mine sounds like Ma's, but I guess it can't be *exactly* like hers.

"We have a wonderful staff team to help you discover and use your voice and other talents. I'll be preparing our actors, and Mr. Jackson will be working with the singers. Ms. Lee will join us for choreography, and parent volunteers will help with costumes, makeup, lighting, sound, publicity, and other essential parts of the production. Oh, and these are our interns, Lily and Tom. They'll be working with us throughout the month. This Wednesday you'll each have about five minutes to sing and act in an audition."

*Wednesday?* In *two* days? That's soon, but I'm not too worried because I have a plan for those auditions. I'm going to sing badly on purpose, just to make sure they don't cast me. I'll have to clue Lily in so she doesn't ask in front of everyone why I sound so off-key.

"The rest of you will stay in the theater and serve as a supportive audience," Ms. Harper is saying. "We'll announce casting decisions on Thursday afternoon. Take it away, Mr. Jackson."

"Your voice is one of your most important instruments of expression," Mr. Jackson says. "We're going to warm it up. Please join me onstage."

Once we're all up there, he leads us in a group hum, which would be embarrassing if I were the only one doing it. Then we try something he calls "the ha," which means we place a hand on our stomachs, push it in and out while saying "ha, ha, ha, ha," and then roll our tongues on the roofs of our mouths to make a *trr* sound. Again, with everyone doing this at the same time, it's not too humiliating.

Lily leads the next exercise—tongue twisters.

"Red leather yellow leather." I get lost after two rounds. Leo's voice is the last to keep going.

The second drill is more complicated: "Whether the weather is cold, or whether the weather is hot, we'll be together whatever the weather, whether we like it or not."

Leo does that one perfectly, too, while I stumble through a few repeats. The good part is that everyone's so focused on trying to get the words right, they're not paying attention to me messing up.

Handsome Tom—I've got to stop calling him that in my head or else it might come out of my mouth—steps up to lead us in something he calls "body practice." He shows us how to roll our necks, shrug our shoulders, circle our arms, touch our toes, and shake out our hands, arms, and bodies. Is this exercise camp or drama camp?

Suddenly, Tom yells, "Be a fried egg in a pan!"

Immediately, Leo falls to the floor and starts flopping around. After a moment, everyone else does the same thing. I get down, too, but I lie still until Leo's sneaker smacks into my foot.

"Sorry," he says, rolling over and smiling. "Stove got too hot."

I don't answer, but I can't help returning his smile.

"All right, eggs," says Lily. "It's mime time. Scramble—get it?—to your feet and find a partner."

Leo turns toward me and we pretend to be stuck in an invisible box. Then we pull each other back and forth with an imaginary rope. This is strange. It's also fun. After a while, I even forget to notice where Jemma is and what she's doing.

When it's time for lunch, Leo joins me in a corner of the cafeteria with his sack lunch. And his guitar. I open my brown bag: Indy's made me a PB and J and thrown in an apple and a couple of the cookies Ms. Maryann gave me.

Lily comes over. "Who's your sidekick, Pandita?"

"Leo, this is Lily. Lily, Leo."

"That your guitar?" she asks him.

"Yep. Would you like to hear a song? My grandfather—who's an opera singer in Manila—says a true musician is always looking for an audience."

I can't believe he's volunteering to play for someone he met a minute ago, but maybe performing is in his genes.

"Sure," says Lily. "There's a guitar scene in *The Sound of Music*."

"I remember," he says.

I do, too. It's when Captain von Trapp and his daughter

Liesl sing "Edelweiss" for the Baroness, but the Captain's eyes keep traveling to where Maria is standing.

Leo gets up, pulls out his guitar, slings it over his shoulder, and starts strumming and singing. "Edelweiss, Edelweiss, every morning you greet me . . ."

Everyone in the cafeteria shuts up and starts listening, including Ms. Harper and Mr. Jackson. Jemma, too, even though she's on the other side of the room.

Mentally, I sing along in the duet I know so well from the movie. His voice is . . . like a cup of sweet, milky tea. No, that simile doesn't work, so I delete the "like." *His voice is a cup of sweet, milky tea.* A metaphor. Yes, that's better. There's only one place where he makes a mistake— instead of "small and white" he sings "soft and white," but nobody else seems to notice.

When he's done, everyone claps. They must be think- ing what I am: Leo's going to get the Captain's part. Girls around the cafeteria are elbowing one another. Looks like a lot of them want to be the future Mrs. von Trapp.

Lily leaves and Mr. Jackson strides over. "That was incredible," he says. "Leo, right?"

My "sidekick" bows. "Yes."

"It's been a long time since I've seen someone so young with your level of talent. You'll be entering high school just when we need a replacement for a strong male singer in our program!" He bustles off, looking delighted.

"What did *you* think?" Leo asks, turning to me. "I saw your face change at one point in the song."

He did? "I thought it was really good."

"Come on, where did I go wrong?"

Words matter, they really do. "There *was* one verse where you changed a word."

"I knew it! The 'soft and white, clean and bright' part, right?"

I nod. "'Soft' makes you think about touch, but the song is about how the flower looks, so the line is 'small and white,' not 'soft and white.'"

"It's all in the details. Thanks for the feedback." He gives me a little bow, which would look odd if anyone else did it, but when Leo dips his head and bends from the waist, it looks . . . right. "My grandfather also says that a musician needs to find the perfect listener in the audience—someone who tells the truth so you can improve."

I catch my breath. What a compliment! I know exactly what he means because I have Mr. Marvin. Just then, Ms. Harper calls us to the back of the cafeteria. I exhale as we walk over, trying not to make it sound like a swoony sigh.

Stacks of white T-shirts and tie-dye materials are spread out on tables. "I've found that wearing the same clothes creates camp unity, so you'll each take home three T-shirts at the end of the day. Wear them to camp daily with jeans, a skirt, or shorts." Her eyes scan the group and land on me. "Overalls are fine, too. And remember, you're all an important part of the musical this summer—whether you end up as actors; set designers; sound and lighting crew; costumes, props, and makeup; or programs and publicity."

Programs and publicity? She's just uttered the best words of the whole day. I might survive this camp if I can work on programs and publicity. *And*, I can't wait to tell Indy that I can wear my overalls after all!

# ELEVEN

AFTER CAMP, I'M GLAD NOBODY else is home. I don't want to tell Shar I'm headed to the Historical Society meeting. Not yet, anyway. After throwing together dinner for myself from leftovers, I practice singing off-key on purpose. I decide to butcher the song "I Have Confidence" for my audition because it's the hardest one in the whole musical. I sure hope Ms. Harper and Mr. Jackson won't be able to tell I'm faking it.

I stop when I hear the garage door open. Baba's late, but there's still time to drive me. Surprisingly, he only asks one question about drama camp.

"How was it, Pandu?"

"I'm still alive," I say.

"That's good."

And that's it. When we stop at a light, he adjusts his tie and checks himself out in the rearview mirror. He's even humming along with a silky song on the oldies station—Baba, who *never* makes music. *Unforgettable, that's what you are. Unforgettable, both near or far . . .* Another strange thing in a long day of strangeness.

Our Chevy Nova rolls to a stop in front of a small ranch house with a big yard in a neighborhood of small ranch houses with big yards. After walking me down the long front path, Baba glances at his watch while I ring the bell.

The door flies open. It's the blonde with the helmet hairdo. "Come in, Dr. Paul," she says. "I'm Margaret. So nice to see you. We'll certainly be glad to have male representation in our Society for once."

Baba takes a step back. "Sorry, I'm not staying. I'll swing back to pick up Pandita. When will this meeting end?"

"Nine o'clock at the latest. The other ladies are much older than I am, so they get sleepy. Not me. Nine p.m. is when life starts for us single people, am I right?" She giggles and pats her feathered hair, which doesn't budge thanks to an astonishing amount of spray.

Baba blows me a kiss, turns, and heads to his car. As Ms. Margaret elbows me aside, he must sense her advancing because he picks up the pace. She chases him down the path, giving up when he leaps in the Chevy and speeds off, like a . . . gazelle escaping a cheetah.

Ms. Margaret returns with a frown. "Maybe he'd like a drink when he comes back to pick you up," she says, leading me inside. "I know how lonely it can get when you've lost a spouse."

"He has the three of us," I say.

Her laugh is as sticky as her hairspray. "That's true, darling, but grown-ups need someone special in our lives, someone our own age."

Maybe *she* does, but not Baba. I shrug. "He's pretty busy with work."

She gives me one of those "adults know best" looks. "You're not old enough to understand, but you will one day."

I hold back my eye-roll and follow her into the living room, where the other Society members are folding flyers and stuffing them in envelopes. I'm a little surprised that my usual "shyness," as Shar calls my silence in public, doesn't descend. Maybe it's because my friend Ms. Maryann is here. Or maybe after our little protest, these four women feel more like comrades-in-arms than strangers, even Ms. Margaret. We all want the same thing: to save the Johnson property.

Ms. Maryann looks up with a smile. "Pandita! How was camp?"

I sit next to her on the couch. "I'm still alive," I say again.

"Well, that's good news. Especially for us. This is Councilmember Mathews and Ms. Margaret. And the redhead in the armchair is Ms. Carol."

"Nice to see you all again." I pick up one of the flyers and read it. SAVE THE JOHNSON ORCHARD! KEEP ONE

OF OUR LAST ORCHARDS BLOOMING FOR FUTURE GENERATIONS! COME TO THE TOWN HALL MEETING THIS SATURDAY AT 10 A.M. AND MAKE YOUR VOTE FOR PRESERVATION HEARD! "Is it really one of our last orchards?"

"Hard to believe, right?" Councilmember Mathews stops folding and gazes into the distance. "If you could have seen Sunny Creek when I was your age, Pandita! Flowering orchards as far as the eye could see. Tourists from all over the world visiting to see them in bloom. Nobody seems to remember that we used to call Silicon Valley the 'Valley of Heart's Delight.'"

I'd never heard that, and I like that name a lot better than "Silicon Valley." I put the flyer I'm holding into an envelope and seal it.

Ms. Carol is shaking her head sadly. "My brothers outvoted me a decade ago when we sold our family's cherry orchard to a shopping mall developer. Bah! That's all we need—more stores and office spaces for computer addicts who get kicked out of their parents' garages."

"This whole area is exporting computers these days instead of fruit," says Ms. Maryann. "I know it's progress, but it's sure hard to see trees cut down."

"What does your father think about giant computers taking over the world, Pandita?" Ms. Margaret, of course. "He's the expert."

"He thinks that one day most of us will have computers inside our homes," I answer, folding another flyer.

Ms. Carol shudders. "Watching us, no doubt. I can't imagine one of those enormous machines whirling away in my living room. Everyone's in such a mad rush to get the newest invention."

"Our state always seems to be in a rush—first we grabbed gold, and now we're grabbing land," says Councilmember Mathews. "When it comes to deciding how the future's going to look in this town, the rest of the Council roars ahead without much thought about preserving the past."

Ms. Maryann clears her throat. Time for a quote, I predict, and sure enough, I'm right. "'How will we know it's us without our past?' John Steinbeck. *Grapes of Wrath*. Preservation helps us remember the good *and* the bad."

"Like the fact that our mothers couldn't vote in this state until 1911, and in this country until 1920," says Councilmember Mathews. "Can you believe it? 1920. That's the year we were born, Maryann."

I do the math: they're sixty. Neither of them seems ancient, so it's weird that they date back to a time when women couldn't vote.

Now Ms. Maryann is turning to me. "I've been thinking, Pandita. The Council is used to biddies like us ranting about saving old places—"

"Speak for yourself," interrupts Ms. Margaret. "I'm no biddy."

Ha! She sounds more like a squawking hen than anyone else in the room. The simile makes me smile.

"Okay, *mature people* like us," continues Ms. Maryann. "But maybe if everyone in town hears from you, Pandita, a young person who cares so deeply about that property . . . well, it might make a difference in preserving it."

My smile disappears. "Sorry . . . I'm not good at speaking in front of strangers. I can't do that."

Ms. Maryann gives me a long look. Then: "Well, we all might have to step out of our comfort zones to win this one. That Golden State Dwellings nonprofit is eyeing the land, and I hear they're flush with donations and young activists."

Including my sister. That rift in the Paul family over this property is coming soon.

Ms. Carol sniffs. "Charlie Reed says they want to build rental housing units over there. Horrible! I'm glad he's on the Council, too. If we can't save the property, he'll make sure we get more retail—not a bunch of cheap rentals."

"Charlie *Reed*?" I ask. "Does he have a daughter named Katrina?"

"Yes, she'll be starting eighth grade in the fall," Ms. Carol says. "Do you know her?"

"Sort of." Can you *know* someone who ignores you? But I don't explain that complication.

"Rentals are a magnet for an undesirable element," says Ms. Margaret. "The two complexes we already have in town are full of drug addicts, welfare bums, and immigrants. Pretty soon it won't be safe for longtime homeowners to walk around this town."

Wait a minute—*we're* immigrants. I hear Shar's voice in my head: *That doesn't sound like preservation to me. It sounds like prejudice.* But I don't say anything.

Ms. Maryann doesn't hold back. "We're not running a campaign to keep people out, Margaret. Who do you think planted those orchards? Immigrants from every corner of the world: Japan, Italy, China, Lebanon, Greece, France, even India—"

"Wait, INDIA?" I blurt out. "I didn't know that! I thought families like ours were the first to come to California from India."

She smiles at me. "Farmers from Punjab moved here long before this country banned immigration from India in 1917. It wasn't until ten years ago that we decided to give visas again to Indians, and only to doctors or other educated professionals like your father."

"That's right, Maryann," says Ms. Carol. "We don't mind hardworking, legal immigrants who come for the American dream, like Pandita's family or that wonderful Mrs. Kim at Orchard Manor. It's the slackers and illegals we have to worry about."

"This entire Valley belonged to the Ohlone first," says Councilmember Mathews. "That means the rest of us are *all* invaders and land grabbers."

Ms. Carol and Ms. Margaret exchange a glance. Looks like there might be a rift in the Historical Society, too.

"My lawyer friend, Sam, who tried to get the property registered as a California Historical Landmark, couldn't get written consent from the property owners, whoever they are," says Ms. Carol. "Their attorneys turned down our request. Sam also said that the Heritage Museum covers the same ground as this property."

We went to the Heritage Museum on a second-grade field trip. I remember an orchard and old houses. Nothing like Ashar Jaiga in my eyes, but I can see how other people might think they were similar.

Councilmember Mathews lets out a deep sigh. "*I* asked the property's attorneys to send over any papers or letters that the owners didn't want to keep. They did agree to that. A bunch of boxes arrived at Town Hall this morning. I have no idea what's inside them."

My heart speeds up. So does my imagination. I'm picturing workers picking up the swing to throw it away. The heavier cushion slips off, so one of the workers unzips it, and voilà!—he discovers some things inside. He doesn't have time to read the letters or look at the photo, so he tosses them into a box along with the other unwanted things. Maybe . . . just maybe, he found my precious keepsakes! Maybe they're inside Town Hall right now!

# TWELVE

"WHAT ARE YOU HOPING TO find, Bev?" Ms. Maryann is asking.

"Anything to prove that the place is worth preserving, but I had no idea they'd send over so many boxes! I had to store them inside the meeting room, and let me tell you, the rest of the Council wasn't happy. The janitor has to clear out that 'garbage,' as Charlie Reed called it, before the town gathers on Saturday. That means we only have four days to search through it, and Bob and I are going to Tahoe tomorrow before the meeting. Can anyone take the lead on this?"

Ms. Carol shakes her head. "Harry and I are heading to the Oregon Shakespeare Festival. Won't be back before the meeting on Saturday, unfortunately."

"Margaret? Maryann?" Councilmember Mathews isn't looking at me.

"I'm allergic to pollen, dander, and dust," says Ms. Margaret immediately.

"I have to work all week at the library," says Ms. Maryann. "But I can try to find out who the owners are.

If we talk to the actual people who are selling the property, not their attorneys, maybe we can convince them to save their family's heritage."

"Oh well," Councilmember Mathews says. "Probably nothing of any historical significance, anyway. I'll tell the janitor to toss the boxes."

Wait, what? No!

I lean forward. "I can look through them."

Ms. Maryann throws me an approving look. "That's wonderful, Pandita."

"There are quite a few," says Councilmember Mathews. "Do you want me to find other volunteers to help?"

If there's a chance in a hundred that my precious things are inside those boxes, I don't want anyone else finding them. "I don't need help, thanks. I'm a fast reader."

"Well, we appreciate whatever you can do," says Councilmember Mathews. "We leave for Tahoe tomorrow evening. Can you meet me in the morning?"

"I have drama camp until three."

"Well, the building gets locked at five, but I guess a couple of hours is better than none," she says. "I'll meet you at Town Hall at three ten sharp."

I hear a familiar beep of a car outside. It's Baba's Chevy Nova. Guess he doesn't want to give Ms. Margaret another chance to pounce by coming to the door. I'm all for that. Calling out goodbyes, I dash outside.

I'm about to plop into the passenger seat when I see that it isn't empty.

There's something there.

Something that doesn't belong to Baba or me.

I pick it up.

It's a scarf.

Purple. Bold. A cottony weave.

Baba pulls it out of my hand and tosses it into the back seat.

"Climb in, Pandu."

I do. But I can't help asking: "Whose scarf is that, Baba?"

"That? Oh, my colleague must have left that behind. I . . . We went for tea. Buckle in, please."

As I fasten the seatbelt around my waist, I take a deep whiff of the unfamiliar perfume lingering in the car. Smells sort of lemony, like the detergent Shar uses to brighten white clothes.

I can't fall asleep that night. A new hum of worry in my mind is added to the roar of anxiety I'm feeling over the Johnson property, Jemma, and drama camp. I can't let Baba's memories of Ma get fogged up by purple scarves and citrus perfume. It's after midnight when I finally fall asleep, and this time my nightmare about standing onstage wordlessly is followed by another—Ms. Margaret, chasing me down the street with a can of hairspray.

# THIRTEEN

LEO WAVES AS SOON AS I walk into the auditorium and pats the empty seat beside him. Every rising-eighth-grade eye follows me—except for Jemma's—and my heart does a little flip-flop as I take the chair.

Lily and Handsome Tom start the day with more tongue twisters, and Leo stands next to me as if he's assuming we'll pair up again. I'm glad because . . . well, now all I have to do is hide in his shadow.

Sure enough, Ms. Harper is watching him closely as we move to another miming exercise. Her bangles clink as she makes notes on a clipboard, and I try to stay out of her sight. She's spending a lot of time focusing on Jemma, too.

Lily introduces a sensory game, and I watch from a distance as my ex–best friend pretends to touch a sharp tack or velvet cloth, taste a sour lemon, hear a loud whistle, watch an imaginary ant move across the floor, and cry while cutting onions. Jemma's so good! Beside me, Leo is acting out the same things, and he's equally good.

Lily comes over. "Pandita! Why are you staring across the room like that? You're supposed to be trying to cry. Look—Leo has real tears in his eyes!"

Oh my goodness, he does. How did he manage that?

Leo smiles and wipes his eyes with his sleeve. "I was remembering something sad. Saying goodbye to my grandparents in Manila."

"Well, it worked," Lily says, and then her face changes. She's thinking of my sad memory, I realize. "Skip the onion, Pandita. Let me see your sour lemon."

That one is easier thanks to the lemons that grow outside my window. I twist my mouth, squint, and swallow.

"Not bad," says Lily, and moves on.

"Who were you staring at before Lily came over?" Leo asks. "David Cassidy?"

He means Tom. "No! Not him. I was watching . . . someone who used to be my friend."

"Oh. I'm sorry. That's hard."

"It is," I say. "So, you had to say goodbye to your grandparents?"

"Yes, when I was—"

Tom comes over and Leo stops talking. "Are you two rehearsing or canoodling?" Canoodling? I've got a decent vocabulary, but I've never heard that word before. I look at Leo; he looks at me. We shrug.

"Let me see you touch some velvet, Leo," says Tom.

Leo complies. As I watch his palm smooth the air

slowly, my worries about the auditions fade away and my muscles relax. I'm starting to get a sense of the word "canoodling."

"Nice work," Tom says. "Pandita, ask your sister to call me tonight, okay?"

"I will." Maybe there's some canoodling ahead for the two of them?

When it's time to break for lunch, Leo and I sit together again. He opens a metal tin of rice and what looks a little like chicken curry, but not exactly. A vinegary, savory smell wafts over the table, and I'm reminded for a moment of the lunches Ma used to make.

"What were you saying about your grandparents?" I ask, unwrapping my PB and J.

"We left the Philippines when I was eight, because Nanay—that's what I call my Mom—got a job offer to be a nurse here in San Jose. We send money and write letters, but we haven't seen my grandparents since we left. Flights are too expensive."

"I know what you mean. My grandparents can't afford to visit, either."

"You're Indian, right?" he asks, and I nod between bites. "Were you born in India?"

"No, here. I've lived in Sunny Creek my whole life."

"I bet this is a good place to grow up. We'd been renting a house in San Jose, but when Nanay got the job at Orchard Manor, we moved to an apartment in Sunny

Creek. It's tiny—only one bedroom, so I have to sleep on the sofa bed. At least for now. My parents keep arguing because Tatay wants to move back to San Jose, where some of our Filipino friends and relatives live."

"Why'd you move here, then? San Jose's not that far of a drive to Orchard Manor."

"A cousin told us that Sunny Creek High has the best music and drama department in Northern California. Nanay wanted me to get to know Ms. Harper right away; that's why I'm in drama camp even though it's so expensive."

Expensive? The amount that Baba wrote on the check didn't seem like a lot. "So, she wants you to be a star. Is that what you want?"

He spoons a big bite of rice and chicken into his mouth, chews, and swallows. "Not a star. Just a really good musician. I like making people happy with my singing."

Oh. That's nice, actually. "You don't get scared performing?"

"Nope. I actually forget about myself when I sing and play. It's like . . . the music takes over my body and mind and I . . . kind of disappear."

I think about this while we both finish another bite. "Sounds a bit like what happens when I'm writing a poem," I say, opening a bag of potato chips. "But not when I'm onstage in front of strangers. Want one?"

He helps himself to a chip. His fingers brush mine,

and I leave the bag on the table between us. It's getting easier to talk to him, even with people staring at us.

"Why are you in drama camp, then?" he asks.

"My father's making me. One of my sisters did this camp when she was my age."

"How many sisters and brothers do you have?"

"Two sisters. Twins, about to start eleventh, like Lily and Tom. Do you have sisters or brothers?"

"Nope. Just me. My father's a biology teacher. What do your parents do?"

This question is the reason I don't like meeting someone new. "Mine's a professor at the university. In the Computer Science department. And my mom . . . well, she died."

There's a silence. Which is okay, because sometimes people follow up with questions I don't want to answer. Like how, and when, and why. After a bit, Leo says: "That's rough."

I'm glad to see Lily coming over, so that we don't have to talk about this anymore. "You need an audition time for tomorrow, Pandita," she says, handing me a clipboard and a pen. "You're the only one who hasn't signed up yet."

"The last open slot is right after mine," Leo says, tapping the blank line.

That's because nobody wants to go after Mr. Talent Show. I sigh and scribble my name under his.

He jumps up, heading for the restroom. "Save me a seat in the auditorium, Pandita?"

I smile. Somehow the way he says my name sounds so . . . much more musical than when anyone else says it.

As soon as he's gone, I turn to Lily. "I don't want a part. You have to convince Ms. Harper that I'll be good at handling programs and publicity. Please, Lily, *please*."

"Sorry, Pandita. This camp's specialty is getting people who don't want to act and sing to act and sing. Besides, girl, you *can* sing. When you sing with Indy and me, you sound great. Just sing like that at your audition."

"I can't. Not in front of a crowd. I'm going to sing off-key on purpose during my audition. Don't let Ms. Harper or Mr. Jackson know, Lily, please."

"I doubt they'll be fooled by a fake bad audition," Lily says. "There's a reason they're considered two of our best teachers. But I won't snitch, I promise."

# FOURTEEN

COUNCILMEMBER MATHEWS IS WAITING outside Town Hall, and she leads me into a large, empty meeting room. Empty, that is, except for a bunch of boxes stamped JOHNSON PROPERTY. DISCARDED BY OWNER. They're organized neatly, with four boxes per pile in six stacks. That's twenty-four boxes, with only four days to look through them—Tuesday, Wednesday, Thursday, Friday. *Yikes.* What have I gotten myself into? I hope Ma's letters and photo are somewhere in this room.

Councilmember Mathews hands me a pair of scissors, tape, and a marker. "Look through as many as you can and set aside anything that seems historically significant. You'll have to repack and reseal the boxes, too. I don't want to create a mess for our hardworking janitor. Mark the ones you've tackled so you don't get confused." She points to an empty box nearby that she's labeled HISTORICAL SOCIETY. "Store anything of value in there. At Margaret's on Friday night, Maryann says she'll look over what you've found. Thanks again for doing this, Pandita."

With that, she leaves, and I'm alone in this big room with twenty-four boxes of dead people's keepsakes. And hopefully, a few of my own. I heave a box from the top of a stack and drop it on the floor with a thud, pull over a chair, and start unpacking.

The box is crammed with inventories of apricot harvests from the early 1900s: sales receipts, spoiled fruit tallies, records of gains and losses. Not "historically significant" in my view, but I sift through them to make sure my letters and photo aren't inside. Somehow I manage to fit everything back in the box, but that takes time, too. Sealing the box, I label it OKAY TO TOSS and haul it to the far wall.

Box number two. More receipts and records. In this one, though, I do notice something kind of interesting. "Anders Johnson, Manager and Owner" signs documents dated 1905, but after 1906, "Lydia Johnson, Manager and Owner" signs them. That was seventy-four years ago. I think back to what Councilmember Mathews said about California allowing women to vote in 1911. This means a woman ran an orchard in Sunny Creek before she could even vote! Was Lydia Mr. Johnson's wife, sister, or daughter? No way of knowing. Not yet, anyway. I put a few of those documents in the Historical Society box.

I keep digging and find contracts with Lydia Johnson's signature next to thumbprints of men named Alfonso Martinez and David Sanchez. It looks like she employed and housed their entire families, a total of six adults and fourteen children. The contracts say that electricity and water will be paid by the landlord. I remember the remnants of indoor plumbing and electricity in the cottages Ma and I used to explore—all those improvements are probably why they seemed much more livable than the tiny shacks for workers on the Heritage Farm. I add the housing contracts to the box of keepers, too.

As I repack the second box, I glance at the clock on the wall. I've only looked through two boxes and it's already four o'clock. Picking up the pace, I sort quickly through the contents of a third box—mostly Sears, Roebuck and Co. catalogs—and repack, seal, and haul that one over to the okay-to-toss section of the room. The muscles I exercised at drama camp are speaking up.

A man's head appears at the door. "You must be Pandita! Councilmember Mathews told me you'd be in here. I'm Señor Alvarez, the janitor. We'll be closing in half an hour."

"Nice to meet you. And thank you!"

*One more box*, I tell my tired body. At this rate, four boxes a day, I'm only going to be able to get through sixteen of the twenty-four boxes by Friday.

This fourth one is heavy. I cut the tape open and pull out descriptions of sulfur treatments that kept apricots a bright orange color as they traveled by train to the East

Coast. These are as dull as reading through the advertisements of water sprayers. I keep hunting, though, hoping to spot Ma's letters or photo, but only unearth endless information about sulfur.

And then, as I'm lifting out the last pamphlet, a yellow envelope—not a lavender one—slips out and lands on the floor.

I pick it up.

The envelope is ancient; the paper thin; the handwriting old-fashioned, with black-inked letters full of curlicues.

It's addressed simply: *For my Beloved Husband Anders, With Love. 1906.*

No stamp, no postmark, no address, but it's sealed.

Finally, something interesting. A letter to Mr. Anders Johnson, the first owner of the Johnson farm, from his wife. And it's never been read.

Should I open it? Part of me wants to. After all, it was in a box that was discarded by the owner, and the person who wrote it is probably dead by now.

But it's written "with love" to someone who never opened it.

Reading what's inside this envelope feels like taking something that doesn't belong to me.

I wouldn't want anyone reading my private letters to Ma, even after I'm dead.

So what to do with this yellow envelope?

I don't want to throw it away, but sharing it with the Historical Society doesn't seem right, either.

Looking around the room, I spot an empty pink carton on a back table. It smells like donuts, and I have to wipe away traces of powdered sugar before putting the unopened letter to Mr. Johnson inside. I'll figure out what to do with it later. For now, the thin, old envelope looks lonely in there. I write PRIVATE, PLEASE DO NOT TOSS on the pink box and tuck it out of sight.

# FIFTEEN

AS SOON AS I ENTER the kitchen, Indy rubs her hands together and cackles like the Wicked Witch of the West. I know what that means. I can smell cheese melting. It's "Tuesday Night at the Movies" at the Paul house. Which means pizza.

"I'll get you, my pretty," Indy croaks in her witchy voice.

Tonight's offering must be *The Wizard of Oz*. That sounds relaxing—exactly what I need. When it comes to movies we've watched again and again, Indy and I practice "a call and response," as she labels it. She starts with a memorized line; I'm supposed to throw the next line back. "And your little dog, too," I answer, matching her screechy tone.

"How was camp?" she asks in her normal voice.

"I'm still alive." It's becoming my catchphrase for the summer.

"I hope you get to play Liesl. Your voice is so high and sweet when you sing."

"No, thank you," I say, pouring myself a glass of water and changing the subject. "Hey, Indy, are you and Tom . . . canoodling?"

"Canoodling? What in the world is that?"

"You know. Do you *like* each other?"

"No. We're just friends. There's no chemistry, Pundit."

"How . . . how would you know if there *is* chemistry?"

"Oh, you usually don't have to ask. It zings through you like . . . like a rash on the inside of your skin."

"Ooh, good simile, Indy!" Does a flutter qualify as a zing?

She lifts her chin. "It *was* good, wasn't it? Maybe *I'll* end up a writer and *you'll* be a star of stage and screen."

"Ugh. No, thanks."

Indy narrows her eyes. "Wait a minute. Why are you asking about chemistry? Is someone making you zing at drama camp?"

My cheeks are suddenly so hot I want to hold the glass of water against them. I shrug instead and try to play it cool. Maybe I've already picked up some acting skills at drama camp? Nope. Indy's still looking at me suspiciously.

Thankfully, the phone rings and she picks it up. I only hear her end of the conversation. "Hello? Oh, hi, Baba. Okay, no problem. Which restaurant? Oooh, that one? It's in the city, right? I hear the chef's amazing. Are you going with a bunch of people? Oh . . ." My sister's one-sided dialogue ends with this: "Have fun, Baba. Pundit and I are eating pizza and watching a movie. See you when you get home."

Indy puts the receiver back in the cradle. "Brace yourself for news, little sister. I think our father's on a date."

That low hum of worry gets louder as I picture that purple scarf. *Inhale, exhale, stay calm, Pandita.* "Did he tell you he was going with . . . a woman?"

"No, but I'll bet you he is," Indy says.

The noise inside me is now as loud as a siren. I'm done with pretending to be calm. I stand up and pound the kitchen table with my fists. "No! This can't be happening!"

Indy jumps. "Pundit! I thought you were on board with helping Baba move on!"

"I never said yes to *that* deal. I want him to share memories of Ma, not make memories with someone *new*!"

Indy hesitates, and her voice is gentle when she replies. "He has to let go one day, Pundit. We all do, even though it's so, so hard."

*Not me*, I think, slumping back onto my stool. *I'll never let go of you, Ma.* But now I don't even have Ashar Jaiga to help me remember.

Indy reaches over and gives one of my braids a gentle tug. "Did you see how uncomfortable Shar got when we talked about ending the pact? It was hard for me, too, when you first brought it up. But I've decided you're right. I'll talk about Ma anytime you want."

I turn to face her. "Really?"

"Yes, really."

I bite my lip and dive in. "Can we start with that day?"

"Which one?"

"The day she didn't come back from the hospital."

Indy sighs, gets up, and cracks the oven door to check on the pizza. It's not quite ready yet. "You're making me start with the hardest memory of all?"

"What happened?" It's more of a plea than a question. "It's such a blur in my mind."

"Okay, then." Indy tries to look casual as she leans against the kitchen counter, but I wonder for a moment if she's using it for support. "Ma wrote me a note once, on one of those lavender cards you like so much. 'It takes courage to perform onstage,' she wrote, 'but it's even harder to be brave in real life.'"

So my sisters got notes from her, too! Maybe one day we can share them. "Be brave now, Indy. Please."

She stands up straighter and takes another deep breath. "Baba told us it was something they call an 'ectopic pregnancy,' which means the baby implanted inside a fallopian tube instead of in the uterus. But nobody knew Ma was pregnant. You were ten, we were thirteen. Most people wouldn't expect a woman with kids that old to be having another baby."

I can't help it; I shudder. The thought of a pregnancy killing Ma is horrible. No wonder my sisters hate talking about it.

But now that she's started, Indy can't seem to stop. "It was such a shock. Ma went to that hospital so suddenly, the doctor seemed sure he could save her, and there we were with Didu and Dadu, waiting and waiting, and then . . . Baba came back alone. It must have been so . . . brutal for him to go through that, and then to have to tell us all. Can you believe he never cried? Not once. At least not in front of us. Not even at the memorial service."

As she talks, the day we were waiting comes back into focus. I picture three girls sitting on Didu and Dadu's sofa, holding hands but not saying a word. Baba, kneeling on the floor in front of us, as if he was asking for forgiveness. Our grandparents, weeping in each other's arms, not caring who saw or heard their grief. I remember the memorial service, too, a couple of months after we came home—Baba rented space to gather a small group at Sunny Creek Presbyterian church. A few neighbors and friends came forward to share memories, including Jemma's mom, but the four of us stayed seated in the front pew.

A smoky smell is filling the kitchen. Indy leaps up and throws open the oven. "Oh, no! It burned!" She flings the tray onto the stove and gingerly tests it with her finger. "The middle's still edible, I think. Let's make the salad."

"I hate that we don't have a grave to visit," I say, tossing the lettuce leaves as she pours the dressing in the bowl. "In the old days, people would visit their town's cemetery once a year on Decoration Day, spruce up their relatives' graves with fresh flowers, and share memories."

"That *is* special," Indy says. "Where'd you learn that tradition?"

"From a book I love—*Emily of Deep Valley*. But Ma's not buried in Sunny Creek Cemetery."

"You're right." Indy cuts off the burned crusts, arranges pizza triangles symmetrically around the edges of our plates, and scoops salad into the middle. "Baba put her ashes in the Ganges River while we were still in India." She pauses and looks off into the distance; her eyes are teary. "I remember *that* day like it was yesterday. It was pouring rain, so the three of us stayed in the taxi."

"I don't remember!" My voice sounds panicky.

She turns to me slowly as if she's coming back to this moment, not in an Indian taxi, but in a kitchen full of the smell of scorched pizza. "Maybe we'll get to it another time."

I take stock of her face and decide to let it go. "Okay. And thanks, Indy, for sharing."

Later, on the couch, with my legs draped over Indy's, and the two of us cackling along with the Wicked Witch, I feel . . . less heavy inside. And based on the way Indy is flinging popcorn into her mouth and missing on purpose to make us laugh, she seems lighter, too.

# SIXTEEN

BY THE TIME BABA GETS back, the movie's over and my sister and I are eating ice cream.

"How was dinner?" Indy asks as soon as he walks into the room.

She's like a dog with a bone. No, a child at bedtime that doesn't want to stop watching television. Long simile, but it fits Indy better.

"Fine. The restaurant was quite good. We had a nice time." Baba smiles and loosens his tie. He didn't say he was with a woman, I tell myself. But there's a smell of citrus perfume wafting around him.

Just then, Shar comes home in her usual rush. "Hey, I've got something I want to show you guys. Join me in the kitchen?"

I rinse out our empty bowls of ice cream and put them in the dishwasher. Meanwhile, Shar pulls a tube of paper out of her bag, unrolls it, and spreads it across the table.

"Take a look," she says.

With her chin on her fists, Indy leans over the paper. Baba does, too. "What's this?" he asks.

"A plan for the property across the street," Shar explains. "We made copies to share so that people in our neighborhood can start to imagine it."

They already have a plan? The Council meeting hasn't even happened yet! I elbow my way between Baba and Indy. My stomach lurches as I take stock of what's on the paper.

It's a colorful, detailed picture of small houses, meandering paths, a garden, a few fruit trees, and a playground. The two cottages along the back of the property—where the Martinez and Sanchez families used to live—are gone, and in their place somebody has sketched a pool and a building labeled "Community Center." The large, sprawling orchard is nowhere in sight. Worst of all, the house—the place where I spent so much time with Ma—has been erased to make space for a new "Property Management Office."

This can't be happening. I won't *let* it happen.

Baba glances at me. I know he's thinking this would be a good time to tell Shar I'm on Team Preservation. But I'm too upset.

"Well, what do you guys think?" Shar asks. "Each rental is a two-bedroom, two-bath unit with a porch and garden—nothing like those tiny apartments in the high-rise rentals at the edge of town."

Tiny apartments? That must be where Leo and his family live, I realize, remembering how he'd described their home.

"I count *forty* units on this drawing," Baba says. "Won't that make for a lot of traffic?"

Shar shrugs. "Some, maybe. But so what? Our street is so quiet now it feels like a cemetery. We could use some younger neighbors. There aren't any young people on the block besides us, and Indy and I are leaving for college soon. Some change would do us good."

It wouldn't do *me* good. "Change isn't always for the better," I say.

"I agree," says Indy. "Where are these new people going to park?"

Shar taps a spot on the paper that seems smack in the middle of the apricot grove. "Here's where the architect wants to put a parking lot. Isn't the drawing gorgeous? We'll make it public once the Council votes on Saturday to permit demolition."

She makes it sound like a done deal.

Baba's nodding. "It's attractive, I have to admit. But I've always liked how that orchard makes our street feel so rural. And I hate to think of the construction noise we're going to have to endure. Well, I suppose we do need some nicer, affordable rentals in Sunny Creek . . ."

Thanks a lot, Baba. So much for Switzerland!

Shar claps him on the back. "That's the spirit!"

"I should probably go to Saturday's meeting to hear the debate," Baba says. "My new colleague might want to come along. She's fascinated by the dynamics between local, state, and federal governments in the United States and how that affects land use and wealth discrepancies."

Indy throws me a look as my heart sinks into my stomach. So that "we" did include a "she."

"Bring her on Saturday, if you want," Shar says. "But the vote to permit demolition is probably going to be unanimous. The zoning battle that comes next will be long and ugly, and probably more interesting for her to observe."

I have no idea what my sister means by "zoning battle," but I don't care. She's not counting the "no" vote from Councilmember Mathews on Saturday. And we might be able to change a few more minds if I find something in those boxes to prove the Johnson Orchard is a historical landmark. "Could be more votes for preserving the property than you think," I say.

"Doesn't matter, really," Shar says breezily. "There's no way the town can afford to buy it."

"Does Golden State Dwellings have the money?" Indy asks.

"We've raised only about two-thirds of the market price, but we're ramping up fundraising and recruiting more volunteers every day. Which reminds me—our office is cramped and doesn't have a kitchen. Baba, think we could meet here on Friday night to plan our fight against those preservation ladies? And Indy, could you make some of your amazing pakora? I'll even clean up the living room."

Now I can't stay quiet. "NO! A bunch of HISTORY WRECKERS aren't meeting in THIS house!"

My sister is silent for a second or two, staring at me, and her expression is shocked. Then: "What's gotten into you, Pundit?"

I take a deep breath. Now or never. "*I* want our town to preserve the Johnson place."

"But why?" Shar's eyes are wide with disbelief. "It's falling down while the town's housing needs are building up!"

"What do you want to see happen there instead, Pundit?" Indy asks. She looks almost as stunned as Shar does.

"NOTHING. I want it to stay EXACTLY THE SAME." I'm still loud—I can't help it.

Shar rolls her eyes. "Well, that's fine, but this is my house, too, and I want to host my team."

Baba puts his hand over mine. "Nothing can stay the same, Pandu. Even though at times I, too, wish—"

Indy breaks in. "Does this have anything to do with that meeting Baba drove you to the other night?"

"Absolutely it does," I say, yanking my hand out from under my father's. "There's not going to BE any

demolition across the street. The Sunny Creek Historical Preservation Society is going to PRESERVE it for the
sake of HISTORY. 'How will we know it's us without
our past?' John Steinbeck. *Grapes of Wrath*."

*Boom.* Mic drop. Thanks for the quote, Ms. Maryann.
And with that, I head upstairs.

# SEVENTEEN

THE NEXT MORNING, WITH MY face pressed against the mesh opening of that horrible new fence, I imagine a young couple buying this place seventy-five years ago. Anders and—*if* she was his letter-writing wife—Lydia Johnson. For a moment, I can almost see them laughing and talking while they plant apricot saplings. I stay there for a while, trying to gather hope that we'll be able to save their orchard. My imagination fast-forwards to 1972, when a slim woman in a shalwar chameez, hair in a long braid, holds the hand of a little girl in overalls as they slip through a secret opening. *Oh, Ma!*

Soon, the sun's position in the sky tells me it's time for drama camp, and this dreaded day of auditions. When I get there it's only 9:45, but most of the campers have arrived already. Leo's sitting in the front row next to Katrina and Jemma, so even though he beckons to me, I slip into a back seat. Slouching, I watch the minute hand on the wall clock. Stupid, stupid time. I want it to move fast today, so of course it creeps along.

Finally it's ten o'clock, and Ms. Harper comes out from her office to give us instructions. "You'll read a scene with me; I'll feed you lines. And then you'll sing with Mr. Jackson accompanying you on piano. Any questions?"

Nobody raises a hand. Anxiety is seeping into every corner of the theater like the smell of burned cooking.

"You have an hour to practice, and then we'll start with our first audition. Katrina, that's you, right?"

Katrina nods. I can see her profile from here; she's gnawing on a fingernail.

"Last chance to prepare, so make the best of it," Ms. Harper says. Suddenly, she shades her eyes with her hand, scans the room, and raises her voice a bit. "Pandita Paul, may we speak in private?"

Wait, what? Me? Why? I shoot a glare at Lily, who shrugs. Getting up, I follow the teacher to a small room backstage. Inside are stacks of scripts and camper application forms. Ms. Harper closes the door behind her. Uh-oh.

"I can tell you don't want to be here, Pandita," she says without any preamble. "Your family made you sign up, am I right?"

I nod. Well, at least Lily kept her promise.

"I want you to know that your sister, Indira, was just as hesitant as you are to perform."

She was? Star of stage and screen, Indy Paul?

"It was a terrible summer for your family, but she threw herself into singing after the first week," the teacher continues. "It comforted her, I could see that. By the end of the summer, she'd discovered the power of art to heal."

I still don't know what to say.

Ms. Harper gives me a long look. "I hear you're a big reader. And writer, too?"

I nod again. "That's why I can handle the programs and publicity, Ms. Harper. I'll do a—"

She holds up a hand to stop me. "Why not use that wonderfully developed imagination to see yourself as Maria von Trapp or one of the other characters in the musical? Write out her thoughts and emotions, and then, when it's time to audition, the words and songs will come easily. Good preparation—and a well-developed imagination—are essentials in acting. Okay?"

I nod for a third time because you're not supposed to argue with teachers. But when she opens the door and leads me back down to the theater seats, I don't take her advice. Instead, I sit in the back row again, watching the others prepare for their auditions and waiting to fail mine on purpose.

The auditions start. As campers go up one by one, I wince when most of them botch my favorite songs. One of the boys, a short blond kid named Joey, manages a decent rendition of "Do-Re-Mi," so I mentally cast him as Rolf. A blond girl named Jenny who sings beautifully would make a perfect Liesl. Katrina has a decent speaking voice, but her singing voice is weak, so I assign her the part of the Baroness, Elsa, a character who doesn't sing.

Now it's Jemma's turn. From the first note of "The Sound of Music," her voice lifts and climbs and takes us to the Swiss Alps. And her acting is good, too. She'll be a perfect Maria. Judging by the looks on Ms. Harper's and Mr. Jackson's faces, it's clear they agree with my casting decision, which means she'll probably play opposite Leo. For some reason, picturing the two of them kissing in a gazebo like the characters in the movie makes me feel strange. I shake off the thought and try to enjoy her beautiful voice.

When Jemma's done, there's an outburst of applause and shouts of "Maria!" I'm clapping, too, hard, and Jemma catches sight of me. She doesn't turn away this time, so I risk a smile.

She smiles back.

*She smiles back!*

I'm so happy I almost forget how nervous I am.

The auditions continue and before I know it, it's Leo's turn. We all knew he could sing after hearing him in the cafeteria, but what's surprising is that he can act, too. His speaking voice projects to the back of the theater, and as he moves and delivers his lines, he somehow morphs into a naval captain. It's amazing to watch a thirteen-year-old Filipino kid becoming the forty-something Austrian

Captain von Trapp. After a stunned silence, he gets an ovation, too, while Ms. Harper and Mr. Jackson exchange looks of glee.

Leo takes a bow, and when he walks off the stage, he comes to the back row to join me.

"Great job, Leo," I say.

"Thanks, Pandita. I love music so much, but I wasn't sure I could act. Ms. Harper's a great teacher. I've already learned so much."

"Pandita Paul," Tom calls out.

I was so focused on listening to Leo, I forgot I was next. Slowly, I get to my feet.

"Give it your best shot, Pandita," Leo says, and his warm copper eyes are full of encouragement. "I'd love to perform with you."

The thought makes me pause for a second. But now I'm heading for the stage. No, forget it. Zing or no zing, I'm sticking to my plan—mumble through the speaking part, sing off-key through the musical part, and torpedo back to my seat.

Ms. Harper hands me the script. She starts to read Captain von Trapp's lines; it's the scene when the new governess first meets the children. In a soft, halting voice, I respond with Maria's answers. People in the auditorium start whispering and rustling. They're louder than I am, and I'm the one who's supposed to be performing.

Ms. Harper spins to face the seats. "Keep it quiet, please. You're a supportive audience, remember?"

She turns back to me. "Don't speak from your throat, project from here." She silences her bangles by pushing her palm on the top of her stomach. "Your diaphragm."

Somehow, I stumble to the end of the highlighted scene in the script. Bad enough. Now it's time to bomb the singing audition.

"Which song, Pandita?" Mr. Jackson asks.

Er . . . "'I Have Confidence.'"

Okay, time to execute my bomb-this-on-purpose plan. But as Mr. Jackson starts to play the first notes, I spot Leo, leaning forward with a smile. He wants me onstage with him; he said so. Jemma's gazing at her hands, which are clasped in her lap. Weirdly, it looks like she's praying. For me? No, that can't be. And then my eyes land on Katrina. She's smirking, probably eager for me to fail. Suddenly, my plan to crash and burn doesn't seem like a good idea.

Because Lily and Indy were right—I *can* sing.

I *love* to sing.

I sang with Ma on the porch swing, I sang with Jemma, I sing all the time with Indy.

With an "aha" flash, I realize, I want Leo and Katrina and everyone in the audience to hear my *real* voice, the one that sounds like Ma's—not the off-key one I'd been planning to use.

"Could you start the song again, Mr. Jackson?" I ask.

"Sure thing. But first, take a deep breath and close your eyes, Pandita."

I do. Then, just as Ms. Harper suggested, I try to picture that I'm in the streets of Salzburg, wearing Maria's shabby dress, carrying an old suitcase and a guitar. Then I let out that breath, inhale an even bigger one, and start singing as if I were in my kitchen with Indy and Lily.

*What will this day be like? I wonder.*

*What will my future be? I wonder.*

When I'm done, the auditorium is quiet. I open my eyes. Everyone's staring at me. And then, to my amazement, Jemma lifts her hands and starts to clap.

Jemma!

Clapping!

For *me*!

Now the whole place is clapping. Even Katrina.

*Even Katrina.*

For a moment, I'm flying.

"Well done, Pandita," says Ms. Harper. "I didn't know you could sing like that! We'll get you acting, too, in no time."

I crash back to earth.

Oh, no.

What have I done?

# EIGHTEEN

AT TOWN HALL, I'M EARLY, so I wait for Señor Alvarez outside the locked meeting room. My head is buzzing with a mix of emotions—fury at myself for not blowing the audition and wonder that I was able to sing so well in front of an audience.

Plus, *Jemma* clapped for me.

Jemma clapped *for me*.

Jemma *clapped* for me.

The words run in my mind like one of the warm-up games we played at camp this week, where we had to repeat the same sentence but emphasize a different word each time. If Jemma and I become friends again, the agony of this camp will be so worth it.

"Hope you find what you're looking for, mija," Señor Alvarez says when he unlocks the door.

From Spanish class, I know "mija" is a term of endearment that means "my daughter." "Yo también, Señor Alvarez." I try out my Spanish, which makes him smile.

I have to get through more than four boxes today.

My letters and Ma's photo will be in one of them, I just know it. But instead, I sort through guides to annual Blossom Festivals, bills from canneries, schedules for cars that carried tourists from San Francisco to the "Valley of Heart's Delight."

Then, when I'm flipping through an old catalog selling "smudge pots," which kept the trees warm during a cold snap, I spot the corner of another yellow envelope. I pull it out of the catalog, along with a folded newspaper clipping. The letter's sealed shut, just like the other one. This one is addressed: *For my Beloved Husband Anders, With Love. 1942. Thirty-six* years after that first one I'd found yesterday, his wife was still sending him unopened letters?!

My finger traces the black ink on the envelope. I want to read what's inside even more than when there was only one, but I stash the 1942 envelope unopened on top of the 1906 one in the box marked PRIVATE, PLEASE DO NOT TOSS. That makes two letters for Anders. But why such a big gap of almost four decades between them?

Carefully, I unfold the ancient, cracked newspaper clipping. It's an article with a headline that reads, "Neighbors Rally to Protect Japanese-Owned Farm." The first paragraph states that after President Roosevelt signed Executive Order 9066 on February 19, 1942, people of Japanese descent, even American citizens, were sent to internment camps. We'd learned about that in school, but it wasn't something I thought about much outside history class. I keep reading. Turns out that while a family named Ichiuji was imprisoned in camp, strangers tried to steal their farming equipment and harvest their fruit. Apparently, the Johnson, Martinez, Sanchez, and some other Sunny Creek families guarded the Ichiuji farm in shifts to keep thieves off the land, harvested the strawberries, and kept the profits safe for the family once the war ended.

A hand-drawn arrow points to the photo of a Japanese couple flanked by mostly white men. There's only one white woman in the photo, and her arm is linked with the Japanese woman's. The caption identifies the couple as Paul and Yutaka Ichiuji and—for some reason I catch my breath—the other woman as Lydia Johnson, widow of Anders Johnson. So she *was* his wife! So that means he was dead by 1942, when she'd written the second letter I'd found.

I peer at the grainy photo. Lydia Johnson was tall and slim, like me, but her posture was confident—shoulders back, crown up, bright smile. *I like you*, I tell the woman in the photo. *I think we might have been friends.*

After a while, I put the old clipping carefully into the box of keepsakes and keep searching. The second box slows me down because it's full of interesting stuff, at least for the Historical Preservation Society. I find three more articles that someone clipped out of newspapers. They're stacked together, just as fragile, cracked, and yellowed as the other one, so I handle them carefully.

The first is dated 1913 and has a strange headline: "Fight Yellow Peril! Keep California White!" Wow. I blink a couple of times to make sure I've got that right. Yep, there it is for real—that unbelievable headline. Horrible. The whole piece, though, has a big handwritten *X* through it and the word *DISGRACE!* scribbled in the margins. I can still read the type underneath the *X*; the opinion writer was trying to convince the government to pass something called the California Alien Land Law, which would make it illegal for immigrants from Asia to own farms. He claimed that the Japanese were stealing the Valley of Heart's Delight from white people. But who drew the *X* and wrote "DISGRACE!"? I can't know for sure, but a closer look leads me to a guess—yes, the hand-written words *could* have been written by the same person who wrote on the envelopes. Lydia Johnson?

The second article is short. It reports that the law passed 35–2 in the California State Senate and 72–3 in the State Assembly. The vote wasn't even close. I'm shocked by how many politicians back then wanted to "keep California white." Do our leaders in Sunny Creek still want this? I remember how Ms. Carol had made it sound like only *some* people should be allowed to live here.

The last of the three clippings is an interview with James Phelan, a man identified as the former Mayor of San Francisco.

*As soon as Japanese coolies are kept out of the country, there will be no danger of irritating these sensitive and aggressive people. They must be excluded because they are non-assimilable; they are a permanently foreign element; they do not bring up families; they do not support churches, schools, nor theatres; in time of trial they will not fight for Uncle Sam, but betray him to the enemy.*

I read that quote three times. Each time, the words land like punches. They make my stomach feel kind of queasy. But then I see that someone has written, *Love Thy Neighbour as Thyself, Mayor Phelan!* in the margins of the interview. And, yes, it's the same curving, bold handwriting! Take that, Mr. Mayor! My insides settle down and I straighten my shoulders. It makes me glad to imagine that my farm-owning, letter-writing woman was against such a hateful law. Should I call her "Aunty Lydia," the way Ma taught us to address grown-up women? It feels more polite, even if just in my own head.

"Tiempo, Pandita."

It's five o'clock. Señor Alvarez has come to let me out. I've found some interesting stuff, but only managed to sort through two more boxes—that makes six marked OKAY TO TOSS. Only two days left. How am I going to conquer eighteen more boxes by Friday?

# NINETEEN

AFTER SAYING GOODBYE TO SEÑOR Alvarez, I walk to Orchard Manor. Mr. Marvin's on the porch, but he's not alone. Leo's perched on the steps, strumming his guitar and singing. Mr. Marvin has his hand over his eyes, and I can tell he's listening intently. Quietly, I make my way to the empty rocker next to my friend.

"A thousand ages in thy sight are like an evening gone," Leo sings. He nods in my direction, greeting me without missing a beat. "Short as the watch that ends the night before the rising sun."

The words are old-fashioned, but I take them in. I think they're saying that my enemy, time, won't get the last word. Mr. Marvin and I listen till the last note, and then he reaches for a tissue, takes off his glasses, and dabs at his eyes.

I'm stunned. I've only heard him laugh—the out-of-control, contagious kind of laughter—twice in the year that I've been visiting him. And I've *never* seen him cry. "Mr. Marvin! Are you okay?"

"My mother's favorite hymn," he says gruffly. "Thank

you, Leo, for singing it so beautifully. You certainly have a gift."

"Thank you," Leo says.

"Sing another?" Mr. Marvin asks.

"If Pandita will join me," he says. "You should have heard her audition. She was so good!"

"She was?" Mr. Marvin raises his eyebrows at me. "Why have I never heard you sing, kid?"

"I don't like singing in public. I'm not sure what came over me at the audition." I *do* know, but right now I'm not letting a pair of coppery eyes talk me into performing again.

Leo drains his icy lemonade in one swallow. "I was just at the library on the hunt for poems to set to my music. The librarian found me a good one by someone named Emily Dickinson. Want to hear that as a song?"

He doesn't wait for an answer or notice that my jaw went clunk. *Emily Dickinson? The library?* Picking up his guitar, he starts strumming and singing.

*I'm nobody! Who are you?*
*Are you nobody, too?*
*Then there's a pair of us—don't tell!*
*They'd banish us, you know.*

For a moment, I'm in my cozy room, listening to Ma's sweet, soft voice reciting that very poem at bedtime.

What good moments those were. But then I return to the here and now, where I'm with a boy my age who likes Emily Dickinson's poetry. Sings with a voice as creamy as afternoon tea. And, for some reason, seems to want to spend time with me. This moment's a decent one, too.

When Leo finishes, Mr. Marvin applauds again. "That happy melody you made up matches the words perfectly. My mother loved Emily Dickinson."

"Mine, too," I say.

"Some poems are perfect to set to music," says Leo. "For me, it's easy to write music, but I sure do have a tough time coming up with lyrics."

"You're looking for poems? Well, I happen to know a brilliant poet." Mr. Marvin ignores my expression of dismay. "Ladies and gentlemen, a poet for the ages—Miss Pandita Paul. Go ahead, kid, recite one of your poems for Leo."

Why are people I love so *pushy*? "Mr. Marvin! That's private!"

But it's too late. Leo's eyes are bright as he turns to me. "I'd like to hear them."

Thankfully, Nurse Corpuz comes out and puts an end to the singing discussion. "Done with my shift. Time to go, Leo. Your Tatay's waiting for dinner."

Leo puts his guitar in his case. "Maybe you can share one of your poems tomorrow, Pandita? I'll sing another hymn for you soon, Mr. Marvin."

"Thanks, kid," Mr. Marvin says. He turns to Leo's

mother. "And thanks to you, too, Alodia. You're revolutionizing this place. Upping the culinary game. Getting Mrs. Kim to hire better workers. And fire the deadbeats, too. About time."

Nurse Corpuz takes a little bow; it looks familiar to me. "Thank you, kind sir. Let's go, Leo. Your father's waiting."

"Bye for now," Leo says, flashing his braces at us.

Rocking in silence, chairs in sync as always, Mr. Marvin and I watch them until they turn the corner.

"That's one fine young man," he says. "I'm glad you've made a friend at drama camp. Other than that . . . what's on your mind, kid? You look beat."

I *am* tired. It feels good to be seen by someone I can trust. "It's that orchard across the street from us. I'm working with the Preservation Society to try and convince the Council that the house and the orchard should be saved as a historical landmark. The town meeting is this Saturday, and it's not going to be easy."

Mr. Marvin puts his empty glass down. "Very few people care about old, broken-down things. Why does a decrepit house matter to a kid like you?"

"Ma and I used to—" I stop. I can't tell anyone about Ashar Jaiga, not even Mr. Marvin. "Ma used to say—" I stop again.

"What? What did she say?"

That the Johnson place felt like home. "That places matter. And so do the people who lived there."

Slowly, he gets to his feet. "Maybe, but they're gone now."

"So what? We still HAVE to try and remember them!" If my voice could project like this in the theater, Ms. Harper would be delighted.

"Calm down. All I'm saying is that this demolition sounds like a done deal. I don't want you wasting your time fighting for a lost cause."

"It's not a waste! And it's not lost yet. We just have to show the Council that it's a town treasure. I've been—"

But he interrupts me, and his voice is gruff. "Time marches on. Nothing we can do to stop it." He starts pushing his walker to the door.

"Mr. Marvin, if you knew how I felt about it—"

The door bangs shut behind him, and he's gone, leaving me on the porch with my mouth open. He's *never* left me like this, alone with an unfinished sentence.

# TWENTY

FOR ONCE, SHAR AND INDY are both in the kitchen eating dinner. My place is set with a covered grilled cheese sandwich on a plate, so I wash my hands and join my sisters. I'm not going to avoid an argument with Shar forever; we still live in the same house. I can't help sighing, though, before taking a big bite.

"You look exhausted, Pundit," Indy says, passing me the bottle of chili pickle. "How did your audition go?"

"Okay." Well, that's a huge understatement. Everything about that audition was . . . complicated.

"And why are you home so late?" Shar asks, as if she's never been late in her life.

I scoop some pickle onto my plate. "Stopped by Orchard Manor."

Another understatement for something that's tangled in knots. I don't want to tell my sisters what I'm doing at Town Hall. Or that Mr. Marvin was so . . . ornery.

"Lily says roles will be announced tomorrow," Indy says. "I can't wait to hear what part you get."

"I'll probably end up doing programs and publicity. Landing a part would take too much time from my *real* summer project—saving the Johnson property." Half a grilled cheese with chili pickle slathered on top has fortified me for battle. I send Shar a hard look that's supposed to pierce like daggers . . . no, like lasers.

"The Johnsons weren't the original residents at that property," Shar retorts. "Even the idea of ownership is relative. Don't forget that Europeans colonized California. Technically, all this land belongs to the Muwema Ohlone people. The Johnsons were just squatters in a long line of squatters."

Dang. She's so good at arguing.

"Try to imagine how it used to be when the Johnsons lived here," I say. "Family farms everywhere. Blossom Festivals in the spring. This area sent apricots, prunes, and cherries everyplace, and the orchards were so beautiful that tourists came from all over the world to visit the 'Valley of Heart's Delight.' That's what they used to call Silicon Valley."

"I didn't know that," Indy says. "'Valley of Heart's Delight.' That's lovely."

"Right?" I reach for my second cheese sandwich triangle and spread pickle across the top.

Shar shrugs. "No matter who named it what, it's not worth preserving those buildings."

But I'm not backing down yet—I can't. "Japanese

116

families farmed some of the orchards during that time, but then a law passed that didn't let foreigners own land. People wanted to 'keep California white,' and there was a lot of hatred of Asians, even after the Second World War. We can't forget that chapter of history, either, right?"

Indy applauds. "Woo-hoo, she scores!"

"You have a point," Shar admits. "Pass the pickle."

I can't help smiling smugly as I hand the jar to her.

"People still want to 'keep California white' in Sunny Creek," Shar says. She takes a big inhale and shoots me a quick look. "I remember when Ma—" But then she stops and looks down at her plate.

*Remember when Ma* what? Keep going, Shar! Suddenly, *I* remember what Ma wrote about me. *Your quiet, listening spirit helps me share things I keep deep inside.* I slow my breathing down and keep my body still. Indy stays quiet, too.

I can barely hear Shar's voice when she starts talking again—Shar, who usually speaks so forcefully! "I remember when Ma tried hard to lose her accent so people around here would treat her more respectfully. After a while, she even stopped wearing Indian clothes except to Bengali parties."

I remember that now, too. She wore Western clothes to the grocery store. Whispered questions for the clerk to me so *I* could ask them for her. Even though I was only seven or eight.

"I remember when Baba got shot at in the garden," Indy says.

My half-eaten grilled cheese falls into the pile of pickle on my plate. "WHAT?!"

"Oh, that's right, you were little, so we never told you about it," Shar says. "Some people back then were mad that Asian-made cars were selling better than American-made cars, so at night, they'd overturn parked Toyotas and Datsuns. That's one of the reasons Baba bought a Chevy. Anyway, one night, a group of teenagers drove by and shot at Baba with BB guns. They missed, thank God."

I can't believe I've never heard this story.

"Ma cried," Indy says. "She and Baba didn't call the police, though, because they didn't want to cause trouble."

"They should have!" I say. "Why didn't they?"

"They worked really hard to be 'American,'" Shar says. "To fit in, and they wanted that for us, too. Why do you think we never studied Bangla or learned how to do Manipuri dances or sing Bangla songs? 'Keep California White' is still around, little sister."

"That makes me sad *and* mad," I say. It's as if hatred from the past swims underwater but keeps . . . coming to the surface . . . no, breaching like a whale.

"I'm glad you're starting to be more aware, Pundit," Shar says. "Sounds like you've been reading that book I gave you for your birthday."

"Mmmm," I say. I haven't opened it, but I don't want

to hurt Shar's feelings. Especially not after she's talked freely about Ma for the first time since I asked if we could revoke our pact.

We hear Baba's footsteps on the stairs, and he comes down to the kitchen. He's wearing a suit and tie . . . wait, is his shirt *ironed*? The odor of musky shaving lotion wafts around him. Well, at least he doesn't smell like citrus perfume tonight. Not yet, anyway.

"You look foxy, Baba," Indy says. "All dressed up for a reason?"

"Going to dinner with a colleague."

"The same one you went to dinner with in the City?" Indy asks. "The one you want to bring to the town meeting?"

It's Baba's turn to sigh. "Okay, here it is. Her name is Dr. Som. Dr. Shefali Som. She's Bengali, like us, an economics professor at Jadavpur University, but she's spending a year here as a fellow. And my department chair asked me to orient her because we 'speak the same language'— even though she's completely fluent in English. So that's what I'm doing. That's ALL I'm doing."

Indy's smiling, but Shar's expression is as shocked as I feel. He's spending time with a *Bengali* woman? This is the worst-case scenario. I could never see him with someone like Ms. Margaret, but someone who can speak Bangla . . . my heart sinks. I can only hope their zing factor is zilch.

# TWENTY-ONE

THE NEXT DAY, MS. HARPER and Mr. Jackson stay holed up in Ms. Harper's office all morning and through lunch. People start muttering about what's taking so long. They're sure, at least, that our teachers will cast Leo as Captain von Trapp and Jemma as Maria. And I can relax once I hear the announcement I want: "Publicity and promotion: Pandita Paul." The words even have alliteration; makes it sound like a done deal in my head.

I glance over at Jemma and Katrina. Jemma crosses her fingers and gives me a little smile. Another one? I almost fall off my chair, but manage to smile back. Maybe, maybe . . . she's on her way back to me? I lay it out in my head: We'll be friend-ish first; we're almost there now! Then, general friends. And finally, we'll be best friends again, just like we used to be. The only problem is Katrina. Are they a buy-one-get-one-free deal? That doesn't sound great.

I'm sitting quietly, as usual, but everyone else starts goofing off due to nerves, so Lily and Tom give up on acting games and pop a videotape of *The Sound of Music* into a VCR. We sit cross-legged on the cafeteria floor in our tie-dyed T-shirts and the other campers sing along to "The Sound of Music." Thanks to Julie Andrews, Lily, Tom, Leo, Jemma, and a few other strong singers, the combined voices don't sound bad.

Next comes the scene at the convent with the nuns. When Mother Abbess sings, only Jemma, Jenny, and Lily can stay with her high soprano. And maybe me, if I were singing, but I'm not. I'm watching the door to the cafeteria. Finally, right as Maria is leaving the Abbey to become the governess for the von Trapp family, Mr. Jackson and Ms. Harper appear and Lily stops the video.

"Okay, campers, we've made our decisions," says Ms. Harper. She splits the sheaf of papers she's carrying and hands half to Lily and half to Tom. "You may take the cast list home along with our rehearsal and performance schedule."

*Please, please, please: Pandita Paul, publicity and promotion.* I channel my message to our drama teacher's mouth.

"Let me warn you: These are final," Ms. Harper is saying. "In a decade of leading this camp, Mr. Jackson and I have never changed our minds. We're not about to start now, even though these were probably some of the hardest casting decisions we've made. Right, David?"

"Right. But that's because we're a little shorter on

singers this summer. Our performance is scheduled for the last weekend of July, so you'll need to start learning your songs as soon as possible."

Lily and Tom start passing out papers on the far side of the room. A silence falls in the cafeteria as people study the list. Then, the shrieks and yelps begin.

"Jemma—you're Maria!"

No surprise there. She'll be amazing.

Katrina flings her arms around Jemma while they squeal and jump up and down.

"Ooooh, look, Katrina, you're the Baroness!"

Hey, that's where I put her, too. More squealing, more jumping from the best-friend party for two on the other side of the room.

"Leo got the Captain!" someone shouts.

Another no-brainer.

"Congratulations!" I say to Leo, who's stayed beside me all morning. "You'll be the best von Trapp ever!"

"Thanks, Pandita! I'm excited to see what you get!"

Lily hands us our copies. Quickly, I scan the list for my name.

There it is: Pandita Paul, Mother Abbess.

*What in the world?!?!*

They want *me* to *act*?

*Onstage*, in front of an *audience*?

No. No way. Mother Abbess is the one who gives

Maria her call to adventure; it's not a huge role, but it's an important one.

"I'm so happy you got a part, Pandita!" Leo taps my paper. "Hey, look, you're also the understudy for Maria! And Joey's my understudy!"

*What in the universe?!?!*

He's right. There it is, right under Jemma Kim's name: Pandita Paul, Maria understudy.

I can't believe this.

I'll have to learn Maria's lines and songs, too? And if Jemma gets sick before a performance, *I'm* the lead?

No. No way.

This can't be happening.

Everyone's talking and celebrating. I catch sight of Jemma glancing around the room. To my amazement, her eyes stop when they find me. She gives me a thumbs-up. Pushing aside my shock, I manage to lift my own thumb in reply.

"I'm so happy you got the Mother Abbess part, Pandita," Leo is saying. "Your singing voice is so good, I thought they might give you Liesl, but Jenny will be good, too."

Joey, the kid assigned to play Rolf (which is how I cast him, too), skips over to Leo and me. We've known each other forever, so it doesn't feel weird when he gives me a hug. He hugs Leo, too.

"Congratulations, you guys!" he says.

"You, too, Joey!" Leo says. "Wait till I tell Nanay that Pandita's going to play the part of a nun. She's going to say it was typecasting because 'that Pandita's such a good girl.' Ha! This is turning out to be such a fun summer."

For him, maybe. For me, not so much. I have to explain to Ms. Harper that my singing yesterday was a fluke, and ask her to switch me to publicity and programs. I know she said she doesn't change her mind, but Shar told me to practice speaking up, right? Well, this feels like the time to start.

I search for our drama teacher through clusters of celebrating campers in the cafeteria but don't see her. Down the hall, the theater is deserted. Or so it seems. As I'm standing in front of the empty first row, I hear voices coming from behind the curtain. And one of them is *loud*.

"I'm sorry, but my casting decisions are final!" This quieter voice is Ms. Harper's.

"But KATRINA is a quarter AUSTRIAN on her father's side!" The loud voice belongs to Mrs. Reed.

"That makes no difference to us," says Ms. Harper calmly. "We cast Jemma as Maria because she has the perfect singing voice and stage presence."

"But—she doesn't LOOK like Maria!"

"May I remind you that none of these children look like the adults they're portraying?"

"I just can't believe you're casting so many NEW-

COMERS! My own mother performed in musicals on this very stage when she was a girl, as did I! And so did many other supporters of your theater program. Well, I can guarantee you THEY won't be donating to the high school program next year . . ."

Mrs. Reed's tirade continues. I can't believe she's threatening Ms. Harper and trying to steal the spotlight from her daughter's best friend. For a moment, I imagine Ma's reaction to Jemma scoring the role: She'd celebrate as if one of her own daughters had gotten it.

Ms. Harper's voice stays calm. "I'm sure Katrina will make your mother proud as the Baroness. You'll see that we made the correct casting decisions once the children perform—that's the magic of theater, inviting an audience to travel with actors across boundaries of time *and* culture into the heart of a story."

"Hmmmph! Good luck doing that with THIS cast! I have half a mind to pull my daughter OUT of your camp!"

I picture Katrina throwing her arms around Jemma and squealing her excitement just a few minutes ago. *Good luck talking her into quitting, Mrs. Reed.*

"That's fine by me," says Ms. Harper. "Katrina seems to be enjoying herself, but of course I'll leave that conversation to you. Now, goodbye."

A manicured hand slices through the divide in the curtain, and Mrs. Reed follows it, storming onstage as if she's making a grand entrance. Or exit, more like. Her high heels clatter down the stairs, and she rushes past me as if I don't exist.

Ms. Harper spots me standing in the aisle near the orchestra pit, and her eyes widen. "I'm so sorry you had to hear that, Pandita. Please don't repeat the conversation to anyone."

"I won't. I promise."

The drama teacher rubs her forehead wearily. "Did you want to see me?"

I hesitate.

*Backstage or onstage?*

I think of Leo's delight over my role. And Jemma, searching the room to connect with a thumbs-up. And then, suddenly, I imagine *my* mother behind me, hands on my shoulders. *Your gift of words will bring joy and hope to the world, Pandu.*

I take in a huge inhale, puff out my cheeks, and let it out. Onstage it is, then.

"Well, Pandita?" asks Ms. Harper.

"I'm leaving a bit early today. I wanted to tell you that I'm volunteering after camp, but that's only for this week."

"I'm glad you won't have to volunteer next week, because rehearsing can be exhausting. You're going to make an excellent Mother Abbess, Pandita Paul, I promise. Keep trusting me, and yourself."

# TWENTY-TWO

I'M TRYING TO MOVE FAST through boxes, but I keep finding interesting items to set aside for the Historical Society—an article about the Johnson Orchard as a tourist stop during a Blossom Festival and a photo identifying Anders Johnson in a group of orchard farmers. I squint at the faded photo. He's stocky and handsome, a perfect fit for Aunty Lydia, in my opinion. The man next to him is a younger version of the Japanese man in the photo with Lydia—Paul Ichiuji again, according to the caption. I notice that one of Mr. Ichiuji's hands is resting on Mr. Johnson's shoulder. Friends. Nice.

Next, there's an article describing the aftermath of the 1906 quake, including a fire at the Ichiuji family's orchard. One line jumps out: "Anders Johnson, owner of an adjoining property, lost his life in a valiant effort to save the Ichiuji barn." Oh, no! So that's how he died! I'm surprised by a small stab of grief. He was so young.

But wait—I'd found an unopened envelope dated in *1942* addressed to him! A warm feeling wells up inside me. So I'm not the only person on the planet who kept writing letters to a . . . departed loved one. Aunty Lydia did, too. She must have taken over the farm when Anders died, which is why she started signing legal documents after 1906.

I keep reading. The article includes a sketch of the Ichiujis' property. I take a closer look and see that it was right across the street from the Johnson trees—exactly where our house is right now! Suddenly, I'm zapped by a jolt of connection to the past. The Ichiuji strawberry farm might have been in our backyard, Mr. Johnson died in a fire nearby, and Aunty Lydia probably mourned him on the same porch where I wrote letters to Ma!

*The letters you're trying to find, Pandita Paul!* I give myself a little shake to get back to 1980. This first box has taken a long time to sort through. Tomorrow, at the end of the day, Señor Alvarez is going to toss everything from the Johnson property. If I don't finish looking through every box, I'll wonder forever if Ma's letters and photo were inside one that I left unopened. The thief of time, as usual, is working harder than I am.

Just as I'm lugging over the second box, the door opens.

In walks Leo. "Hi, Pandita."

I drop the box on the floor in front of my chair. I'm too surprised to be polite. "What are *you* doing here?"

"A bunch of us wanted to get ice cream after camp to celebrate the casting decisions, so I popped into the library to find you. Ms. Maryann told me that you're volunteering here. She said you needed help searching through boxes?"

Ms. Maryann! Why?! "Really? I told her I could handle it. You don't have to stay."

He doesn't answer. Instead, he walks around the room, looking at the stack of boxes marked OKAY TO TOSS on one side and the unopened boxes against the opposite wall. "She said you have till tomorrow afternoon to look through all of these?"

I plop down on the chair with a sigh. "Yep. And I have to repack each one and reseal them so I don't make more work for Señor Alvarez, the janitor. But I'm the only one who knows what to look for, so I don't know what you could do."

"I could move boxes and repack them. Besides, I have to hang around somewhere until Nanay gets off work."

Well . . . accepting his offer might be the only way I'm going to get through every box by tomorrow.

"Okay, then, you can help. We keep anything that might convince the Town Council to preserve the orchard that's across from my house. I'm putting stuff like that in here." I point to the box marked HISTORICAL SOCIETY.

"Sounds good." He goes to get a chair, sets it down opposite me, and hauls a box over.

But how am I going to explain that I'm also looking for my own keepsakes? I think for a moment about how to word this. "And . . . if you spot lavender OR yellow envelopes, *please* don't open them—just tell me and I'll take it from there."

I brace myself for curiosity, but all he says is: "Will do. Mind if I turn on a radio? Music helps me concentrate."

"That's a good idea. My sister does the same thing while she's cooking."

He grabs a small, battery-powered radio from his bag, pulls up the antenna, and tunes it to the top hits station that Indy likes. Soon, he's singing in perfect harmony to "It's Still Rock and Roll to Me" by Billy Joel as we rummage through boxes. After a while, I start singing along. He's right—music does make this seem less like drudgery. Every now and then he stops singing to ask if something's significant, and we consult, but with both of us working, we're moving through boxes twice as fast.

After a while, though, Leo suddenly switches off the radio.

"Yellow envelope," he says quietly.

I walk over. Sure enough, on top of a pile of newspapers and faded receipts in the half-empty box is another sealed letter. This one is addressed: *For my Beloved Husband Anders, With Love. 1956. Fourteen* years after the second one I found, and *fifty* years after the first one. Wow, Aunty Lydia. You stayed faithful.

Carefully, I pick up the letter and carry it to the donut box.

Leo's following me, and he peeks over my shoulder. "You found two others? Did you read them?"

"I can't. They feel so *private*. Do you mind not saying anything about them, not even to Ms. Maryann? I'm hoping we find out who owns the land. If it's someone related to Anders Johnson, I'll hand over these letters."

"I'll keep them a secret, I promise. Who *was* Anders Johnson, anyway?"

"One of the people who planted the orchard we're trying to save."

"What else do you know about him?"

I hesitate. "We need to keep looking. Besides, do you really want to hear about a stranger who died a long time ago?"

"Absolutely," he says. "We'll keep working while you talk."

So I tell him everything—about the big earthquake, the Ichiuji family, and the fire that took Mr. Johnson's life. I describe how Aunty Lydia—"Mrs. Johnson" for Leo's ears—took over the orchard as a widow, stood up for their neighbors against those "Keep California White" people, hired two Mexican families to help her, and maintained spacious, comfortable cottages for them on the property. I see her in my mind's eye as Leo listens. She's in a calico dress and an apron, hanging clothes on a line while she calls out directions to harvesters picking apricots. ". . . and now the Council's going to decide whether or not to preserve that place or let the owners demolish it."

"Mrs. Johnson sounds so brave," Leo says. "Listening to you makes me want to save her property, too."

Señor Alvarez pops in. "Found a helper, Pandita?"

"Another volunteer," I say. "This is Leo. Leo, Señor Alvarez."

"Good, because your time's almost up. Think you'll be done by tomorrow afternoon?"

I look around and do a quick count. Wow, with Leo and I both working, there are only six boxes left to open! My treasures *have* to be in one of those. "I think so. I'll try, anyway."

"*We'll* try, you mean," Leo says. "I'll come back tomorrow, *and* I'm going to that Council meeting. Now, I want to save the Johnson property, too."

I beam at him.

The box for the Historical Society is almost full, so Leo and I lug it to the library for Ms. Maryann to look through.

"I have to run," Leo says, after the box lands on Ms. Maryann's desk with a thud. "Nanay's shift ended twenty minutes ago. See you tomorrow, Pandita! Bye, Ms. Maryann!"

I watch him go; I can't help it. Ms. Maryann watches

me watch him go. When I turn back to her, she's smiling. I am, too.

"How's the archeological dig?" she asks.

"A little better now that I have company. Thanks, Ms. Maryann, for sending Leo over."

"Thanks for accepting the help. 'I can do things you cannot, you can do things I cannot; together we can do great things.' Mother Teresa."

Dang. How does she come up with perfect quotes so quickly?

"Did you find out anything more about the Johnson family?" I ask. "Did they have children?"

"Yes. One son, born in 1906."

"What? That's the year of the big earthquake! That's when Mr. Johnson died!"

"I knew you were a historian, Pandita! I hadn't made that connection. Anyway, there's no record of any other children, as far as I can tell. Anders is buried in our cemetery, but there's no record of Lydia's death, at least not in California."

"Could she still be alive?" I picture myself handing three unopened envelopes to an ancient version of my imaginary Aunty Lydia.

"I doubt it. She'd be over a hundred years old. Besides, there's no trace of her residing anywhere else in the state."

The picture in my mind shifts; now I'm handing the

letters to Aunty Lydia's descendants. "What about their son?"

"He must have been baptized here in Sunny Creek at the same Lutheran church where they were married, but I couldn't find a baptismal certificate. There's no public record of his death, either, and nobody by that name and age in the county or state."

"So how can we find him?"

Ms. Maryann closes her notebook with a sigh. "I have no idea. Also, my friend Consuela said there's nothing the Ohlone can claim for preservation on the property. Except every bit of soil, of course. She's volunteering at that nonprofit because affordable rentals might be the only way some members of the Ohlone Tribe can afford to live in Sunny Creek." Her shoulders slump ever so slightly. "Pandita, I don't think we're going to win this one."

"What? No! We can't give up, Ms. Maryann!"

I can't bear the thought of those machines tearing down the Johnson home and uprooting their beautiful trees. And what about me? I can't lose Ashar Jaiga.

"Well, we'll talk about it at our meeting. I'm so tired. I think I'll head home early."

# TWENTY-THREE

WHEN I TELL THE FAMILY that I got the role of Mother Abbess, Indy whips up cupcakes, and Baba and Shar join in the celebration, with Shar trying not to look smug as we toast my "dramatic success," as she calls it, with glasses of sparkling cider.

Baba clears his throat. "Shar, would it be okay with you if . . . May I invite Dr. Som to come here for your meeting tomorrow? I think I mentioned that housing and land-use issues are her specialty."

Shar swallows, hard, and throws Indy a desperate look; Indy gives her a nod of encouragement. *And* probably a kick under the table. "Um, okay, Baba," Shar mutters, and then her voice returns to its normal volume. "But we're focusing on action, not more discussion."

I feel a flash of solidarity with her; sounds like she doesn't like the idea of Baba "moving on" with someone else, either.

"Well, I for one can't wait to meet Dr. Som," Indy

says. Her toes find my shin under the table again. "How about you, Pundit?"

I pull my leg out of reach. "I have my own meeting to go to on Friday night. Baba, can you drive me to Ms. Margaret's again? You promised, remember?"

"Sure, Pandu. I'll drop you off on my way to pick up Dr. Som. And then I'll run back to get you at nine. Unless maybe Ms. Maryann can bring you home?"

"I'm sure she can."

"The Historical Society meeting ends at nine?" Shar smirks. "That's right—old people don't stay up much later than that. Our meeting's *starting* at eight. You'll be back in plenty of time, Pundit." So much for sister solidarity.

"Great!" says Indy. "We can ALL meet Dr. Som, then."

Ugh.

At camp on Friday, after some more tongue, breath, and movement exercises, Ms. Harper splits us up into five groups that will "contribute equally to the musical's success." Our first task is to choose a group name. The actors pick "Team Hollywood," which I think sounds a little full of ourselves. I'd thought of "The Gong Show," a talent show on television about wannabe actors, dancers, and singers who get gonged by judges, but I don't say it out loud. The second group, a few happy-looking set designers and painters, call themselves the "Van-Go-Getters," which is much more creative than our choice. The sound and lighting crew, all technology lovers, label themselves "Silicon Valley." Costumes, props, and makeup choose "Vogue." And "Playbill," a group of three, will handle programs, ticket sales, and advertising.

A few mothers are volunteering to help the non-actors, so they lead their students into different classrooms. I can't help looking wistfully after Playbill. It would have been so easy to be a part of that group. Team Hollywood is the largest group; I count a dozen of us who walk to the cafeteria for our next session.

A young woman is standing next to Ms. Harper and Mr. Jackson. "This is Ms. Lee," Ms. Harper tells us. "She's a choreographer; she's going to stage your movements and teach you the dances required in this musical."

There's a dead silence. I picture the romantic dancing in the movie version. How's that going to work with kids our age? Jenny-Liesl is a foot taller than Joey-Rolf, but they don't seem worried at all. In fact, they're already trying to waltz around the cafeteria.

Leo slowly raises his hand. "Ms. Lee . . . I'm not that good at dancing."

Ms. Lee steps forward. "Not to worry," she says. "I will keep it very simple. No gazebo dances. No kissing, either." That gets a couple of giggles. "Just a short waltz for everyone and a folk dance called the ländler for Maria and Captain von Trapp. Also, the 'Do-Re-Mi' and 'So Long, Farewell' choreography for the children."

I'm relieved there won't be any romantic gazebo dances. But that Austrian folk dance scene is still kind of steamy, at least in the movie version. Wait—does Pandita-understudy have to learn to dance with Leo, too? With everyone watching?

Joey stops trying to waltz alone and asks the question I'm thinking, but in reverse. "I hope I get to learn both dances?"

"Of course," says Ms. Harper. "You're the understudy for the Captain, so you'll be ländlering and waltzing in no time. And you, too, Pandita. You will all surprise yourselves. I've seen Ms. Lee teach a football player to do a perfect pirouette."

Suddenly, a memory comes to me: Ma performing a Manipuri dance at a Bengali gathering after Baba talked her into it. I see her in my mind's eye: quiet; elegant; jasmine flowers woven into her braid, hands, feet, and hair; moving in perfect rhythm to the music. And Baba, watching with adoration in his eyes. Could I have inherited some of that talent? I sure hope so.

"Let's start in a circle," says Ms. Lee. "Dancing is about communication, respect, courtesy, and elegance. Without spoken words."

I'm standing between Leo and Joey, with Jemma on

the other side of Leo and Jenny on the other side of Joey. Ms. Lee asks us to turn and walk in the circle single file in a one-two-three movement, with one a long step and two-three a shuffle movement that switches our feet. I get it quickly, faster than everyone except Katrina, who's waltzing like her Austrian ancestors might have waltzed. I'm following Leo, and at first he's stumbling, but as we keep going, he gets a bit better at the rhythm.

Soon, we're all sweating like we're in a jungle instead of an air-conditioned cafeteria. Leo's T-shirt has dark circles under his arms.

"One-two-three, one-two-three . . ."

Behind me, Joey is humming "My Favorite Things" under his breath.

Ms. Lee overhears him. "That's a perfect song for the waltz, Joey. David, could you give us a slow rendition of 'My Favorite Things' on the piano? Now, let's try this one-two-three movement backward, shall we?"

With the music, it gets even easier. At least for me. Ms. Lee smiles as she passes me. "Nice work, Pandita."

Thanks to Ma's genes, I *might* survive the singing and dancing parts of this musical. Now if only I can live through the speaking and acting parts.

At the end of Ms. Lee's first lesson, we head back into the auditorium. Tom holds his nose as we pass him. "Deodorant, please, eighth graders. Tons of deodorant, all summer long."

Ms. Harper hands out scripts. "Shall we begin with just the spoken parts first? Mr. Jackson will work with you on the songs in the afternoon."

I'm onstage with the other nuns in the third scene. I'm the first to speak in this scene, but I can't seem to make it through my line without my voice fading into a murmur. Ms. Harper takes me aside, showing me how to take breaths at the right times and pronounce each word distinctly. I do okay with her. But back onstage with everyone watching, my voice dwindles into nothingness again.

"Well, we'll keep working on it, Pandita," Ms. Harper says.

"Don't worry, Pandita," Leo calls out. "You teach me to dance, I'll teach you to project."

My cheeks feel warm as I take in the sight of Jemma grinning up at me from her seat. Our friendship, apparently, is returning with nonverbals first.

Mr. Jackson tells us to take it from the top of scene two. "Nuns, get up here please. Just the song. No spoken lines needed, Pandita."

With Leo's and Jemma's faces in the audience bolstering me, I belt out the song "Maria" with the four other girls who are playing nuns. I've sung this at least a dozen times with Lily and Indy at home, so I know it by heart.

Mr. Jackson seems pleased. "Nice work, nuns. Next scene: Maria, singing 'I Have Confidence.'"

Jemma's so, so good, I think. When she's done, I get up and walk over to where she and Katrina are sitting.

"That was wonderful, Jemma," I tell her. "You're the perfect Maria."

She hides her surprise like the good actor that she is. "Thanks, Pandita. You were good, too."

We've graduated to words. My heart literally wants to sing with the sound of music.

# TWENTY-FOUR

AS LEO AND I WALK to Town Hall, I know this is my last chance to find my keepsakes.

"Thanks again for helping," I say as we climb the stairs that are starting to feel familiar.

"Walang anuman," he answers. "That's 'you're welcome' in Tagalog."

"It's cool you still speak it. I can only remember a few words in Bangla."

"That's kind of sad."

"I know." Maybe after I get my family to start talking about Ma, I can convince Baba to teach me more Bangla.

Inside the meeting room, Leo switches on his radio and we get to work. In the first box he opens, he finds a fourth yellow envelope almost right away. "ANOTHER ONE!" he shouts, and I race over. This one is addressed: *For my Beloved Husband Anders, With Love. 1924.* For some reason, my eyes sting a bit as I hold the envelope in my hands.

Leo's quiet, too. Then: "Feels sort of magical to find these after so many years."

I put the envelope in the box with the others. "It is. Wonder if she wrote more than these four." I have a feeling she did—my guess, given my practice, is at least one a year.

Suddenly, the door swings open. Standing at the entrance to the meeting room are Mr. Reed and Señor Alvarez.

Mr. Reed looks around the room. "This has to be cleared out right now, Luis. I've scheduled a meeting in here at four."

"As I told you earlier, sir, Councilmember Mathews told these kids they could be here until five," Señor Alvarez says, sending me a sympathetic look.

"Don't worry about Bev. I'll handle her. Kids, clear out of here right now and go enjoy your weekend."

The door bangs shut behind him. I can't believe this. I thought we had two hours. Panic is rising in my throat; what if my stuff is in one of the boxes that we haven't searched yet? I turn to Señor Alvarez, who's scowling at the door. "May we keep looking for a while longer?"

"You heard the order—I'll have to get this place completely clean by four." He looks at my face. "Tell you what, mija. I'll bring in a couple of empty trash cans. That way, you two can keep looking and toss boxes away directly into the bin. In the meantime, I'll be hauling out the boxes you've repacked so neatly for me. We'll all move like lightning. Does that sound good?"

"That would help a lot. Oh, wait! There's some stuff I'm taking with me. Let me get that out of your way."

I take the four yellow envelopes out of the donut box and tuck them into my bag. Then Leo and I get to work on the last boxes, backs bent, fingers flying. Not having to repack the stuff does help. Once Señor Alvarez has hauled everything we've inspected out to the dumpster, there are only two unopened boxes left. My letters and photo have to be in one of these, they just have to.

"Please, five more minutes?" I ask Señor Alvarez.

He sighs and looks at his watch, but nods. "Make it quick."

I turn to Leo. "Forget everything else—just look for lavender envelopes!"

"And yellow ones?" he asks.

"Those, too."

While Señor Alvarez sets furniture up for Mr. Reed's meeting, Leo and I tear open the last boxes, rummaging and tossing as if we're competing in an Olympic box-searching event. All I want to find are letters from Ma to me, letters from me to Ma, and one fading photograph of a girl in an Indian village. Is that too much to ask?

Señor Alvarez is vacuuming now, and the roar of his machine fills the room. As I reach the bottom of my box, I'm fighting back tears. Nothing. I look over at Leo, but his box is already empty, and he's carrying the contents to the trash cans.

"No letters in this one, either," he says. "Lavender *or* yellow."

I can't believe it! After all this work, not a sign of my keepsakes. They're long gone by now, dumped in a landfill or incinerated. Leo takes a look at my face, picks up the pile of useless items that were in my box, and dumps them in the trash can. He doesn't ask why I'm crying.

Señor Alvarez walks over with a box of tissues. "I'm going to tell Councilmember Mathews how Mr. Reed kicked you out of here early."

I take a tissue and blow my nose. "It's okay. We got through the boxes at least, thanks to both of you."

Señor Alvarez pats me on the shoulder, and Leo helps him wheel the trash cans out to the dumpster. After we all say goodbye, I pick up my bag with the four letters and trudge home.

My family is running around getting the house ready for the Golden State Dwellings meeting. Shar and Baba are setting up chairs, and Indy's mixing a batch of pakora batter. All the clutter in the living room is gone. I can't believe this is what it takes to get them to clean up! I walk around making adjustments so that photos of Ma are still on display, front and center. I want *that woman* to see their wedding photo, with my beautiful Ma in a red saree standing right beside Baba, both of them garlanded in jasmine.

When Baba drives me to Ms. Margaret's house, his Chevy still smells of that citrus perfume. Yuck. Rolling down the window, I don't ask him questions, and after a couple of sideways glances at my face, he doesn't ask me anything, either.

Only two others are in attendance at the Historical Society meeting—Ms. Maryann, who tells Baba she's not feeling well but she'll drive me home, and Ms. Margaret, who has to be there because it's her house. I picture the dozens of chairs waiting for Shar's team inside our home. Team Preservation is now down to three members? We're doomed.

"Carol and Bev are still on vacation," Ms. Margaret explains. "But don't worry, I'm sure Bev will be back in time to cast her vote tomorrow afternoon."

Ms. Maryann's face looks flushed. "I have a sore throat so don't come too close," she warns, taking a sip of steaming tea. "Did you learn anything new about the property today, Pandita?"

"Not much; we had to race through the last boxes because we got kicked out early. Did you look through the box keepers, Ms. Maryann? Lydia Johnson was amazing, right?"

Ms. Maryann rubs her temples with her fingers. "I was

so tired yesterday, Pandita, I didn't have the energy. Why don't you just tell us what's in there, in your own words?"

I share the Johnson's story just as I did with Leo. By the time I tell them about Mr. Johnson's death in the fire and how his widow fought for the Ichiuji family to keep their property, Ms. Margaret is teary-eyed.

She dabs at her eyes with a lace-edged hankie. "I can't believe her husband died so soon after they were married! It's called the Great San Francisco earthquake, so we forget that it did damage all the way down here."

"So lovely to hear a young person talking about the past," Ms. Maryann says. "You know, Pandita, if you stood up in that meeting tomorrow and told the Johnson family's story, talking as freely and expressively as you did now, we might have a shot at changing some minds. 'The tongue can paint what the eyes can't see.' Chinese proverb."

Even at the thought, my voice flattens and softens. "I can't do that, Ms. Maryann. Maybe I can write something for you to read?"

"It matters greatly *who* says something," Ms. Maryann counters. "The container of an idea is as important as the idea itself, if not more so. Please, at least think about it. But I guess I can read your piece if you can't muster the courage."

At that, she gets up to go. "I'm sorry, ladies, I need to rest. Come on, Pandita, I'll drive you and this box of stuff to your house."

"Now? But . . . it's not even eight o'clock!" Shar's meeting will be starting by the time I get back. Baba probably still hasn't even returned home with *that woman*.

"Aaaaachoooo!" Ms. Maryann sneezes into a tissue and heads for the door.

We don't talk much on the drive. A long row of cars is parked in front of our house, so Ms. Maryann pulls into the driveway. "One of your sisters having a party?"

I sigh. "No. I've been meaning to tell you. My sister Shar works for Golden State Dwellings, so they're having a meeting at our house. Can you believe it? They're in there right now, planning how to destroy the property."

Ms. Maryann gives me a little nudge with her elbow before I get out of the car. "Maybe you can spy on them for a bit? Might be helpful to find out what they're thinking."

I sneak in through the back door, lugging the box of Aunty Lydia's remnants. Indy greets me absentmindedly, applies lipstick, and heads to the living room carrying a plate of pakoras. Loud voices and laughter do make it sound like a party out there.

I drop the box on the kitchen table with a grunt. I'm so tired of boxes of old things. What good are they? Well, I'll haul this last one upstairs and write up something for Ms. Maryann. But first, a little spying is in order.

Standing at the living room door, I survey a crowd of about thirty people. A man wearing a blazer and tie with skin almost the same color as his short afro is talking by the fireplace. His audience is mostly young and bursting with energy. My heart sinks. How are four older ladies and one kid supposed to compete with this group of powerhouse activists?

"We'll split up into subcommittees again, but first I want the whole group to hear updates," the man is saying. "Subcommittee one—defeating those preservation folks to get that property and orchard demolished and cleared for sale. Tomorrow's the Council meeting. Are we ready?"

Subcommittee one sounds like enemy number one, so I flinch when Shar raises her hand. "Good news from the civil engineers," my sister says. "All buildings on the property are structurally unsafe and infested with termites. And the arborist's report confirms that ninety percent of the apricot trees are diseased—some kind of soil problem, I guess."

That glorious apricot orchard? Diseased? No way! Aunty Lydia's house? Infested? Never! But my hopes are sinking; civil engineers and arborists probably know more about buildings and trees than I do.

"That's good news," says the man by the fireplace. "Looks like tomorrow's vote for demolition, at least, is going to be an easy win. But we're headed for a contentious debate down the road over zoning. Consuela, what's the word on that?"

The only middle-aged woman in the room stands up. Unless there's another person named Consuela in town, this must be Ms. Maryann's friend—the Ohlone leader.

"Reed and McDermott are buddy-buddy with commercial office developers," she says. "They'll likely vote to change the zoning in this neighborhood to multiuse and knock our offer off the table as well as the ones from residential developers. The mayor and Councilmember Bailey seem to favor keeping the single-family, low-density zoning that's already in place, which blocks both the office developers *and* us. Oh, and Councilmember Mathews is still trying to preserve the property, but once that's not a possibility I think she'll vote with us to change it to multi-family zoning."

Suddenly, there's a sharp tap on my shoulder. I jump.

"You must be one of Anand's daughters!" declares a loud voice with a lilting accent.

Standing behind me is a stocky woman with curly hair and skin the color of an oak trunk. The crinkles in her round face remind me of bark. Dr. Som, of course. Here she is, smiling smugly up at me, wearing that bright purple scarf and clogging up our entire kitchen with a spritzy odor she must think is perfume.

# TWENTY-FIVE

SHE HAS TO LOOK UP at me because she's about the same height as my sisters in bare feet. Well, at least she's taken off her shoes; everybody in the living room still has theirs on.

Baba walks out of the small bathroom by the garage door. "I see you've met Pandita, my youngest." *My?* Why not "our"?

Indy comes into the kitchen carrying empty plates. "Oh, hello. Good thing I put more pakoras in the oven."

"Looks like they were a hit," Baba says. "Indira, this is Dr. Shefali Som. Shef, this is my middle daughter."

"My" again. And why is he calling her "Shef"? He's given her a nickname already?

"May I?" asks The Intruder—*my* nickname for her. She's pointing to a pakora that Indy's sliding off a cookie sheet.

My sister puts it on a napkin and hands it to her. "Of course. I hope you like it. I used our grandmother's recipe."

The Intruder chews and swallows. Then: "It tastes

*something* like our pakora in Calcutta, but . . . did you fiddle with the recipe?"

Indy's eyes widen. "Well, I added some—"

The Intruder interrupts to finish the sentence. "Things that make these taste *very* American. I'm sorry, but I can't tell you how to fix it. 'Shef' is definitely a misnomer of a nickname. I'm no good at cooking, only excellent at eating."

Our unwanted guest throws back her curly-haired head and laughs loudly at her own joke. When Baba joins in, though, I almost fall over. I can't remember the last time he laughed like this. I look at Indy; her eyes are wide.

"I'm certain these American guests won't know the difference," The Intruder is saying. "Shall we go into the meeting, Anand? It sounds as if they've already started."

They leave the kitchen. I turn to Indy. "Still happy about this?" I ask.

She shrugs. "Not about the cooking critique, but Baba seems to like her, and that's what matters."

Indy hands me a plate and a stack of napkins, and I follow her into the room. People reach for pakoras immediately.

"I'm pleased to introduce Dr. Shefali Som," Baba is saying. "Dr. Som is an economics professor at Jadavpur University in Calcutta and has just completed a year doing research on land use in the Soviet Union. She's very interested in your plans for the Johnson property."

"I am indeed," says The Intruder. "Would it be permissible to stay and listen?"

"Of course," says the man who'd been leading the meeting. "I'm James Flemming, by the way. Executive Director of the Santa Clara County chapter of Golden State Dwellings."

"Do you live in Sunny Creek?" asks The Intruder.

"I live in East Meadow, about five miles away," answers Mr. Flemming. "A lot of Black people can't afford to buy or rent in Sunny Creek because housing is so expensive."

I'm a little surprised that I'm not surprised. I've known my whole life that East Meadow is a mostly Black town. As Shar likes to point out, most Sunny Creek residents are white, unless you count the apartment building on the far edge of town where Leo and his parents live.

Baba and his "colleague" squeeze into a space on the couch meant for one person. My heart plummets as I register how Baba is gazing at her—as if she's the only one worth looking at in the entire room. They're sitting so close her stupid scarf is splayed across the front of his suit. Disgusting.

"Research subcommittee," Mr. Flemming is saying. "Julia, any progress on finding the owners of the property?"

A lanky, red-haired, freckled woman wearing a T-shirt with the university's logo raises her hand. "The lawyers for the trust are keeping all identities secret. We're at a bit of a dead end."

They won't be able to out-research Ms. Maryann. If she can't find information about the owners of the property, nobody can.

"Don't give up," says Mr. Flemming. "We're raising good money to come up with a competitive offer, but our best hope might be making a heartfelt appeal to the seller."

The Intruder whispers in Baba's ear and then bends her head back in that same annoying bellow of a laugh. Baba's chuckling, too. Or wait—is he *giggling*? My insides are boiling; I can't stand the sight of this happening inside my home. Ma's home, the one that *she* decorated, that *she* cleaned, that *she* loved. I hope Baba's eyes land on the wedding photo, but *that woman*'s head is probably blocking it from his view.

The plate I'm carrying is only half-empty, but I back into the doorway between the living room and the kitchen. Voices are louder now; people are interrupting one another. They're arguing over how much money to charge tenants if they actually do manage to buy the land and get the zoning changed. Shar's in full debate mode; she's pushing to apply for government subsidies which would allow them to offer lower rents.

A voice rings out from the other side of Baba. "You sound like Russian communists. What a disaster I saw in that country!" The volume of her comment brings other conversations in the room crashing to a halt, but The Intruder keeps going. "Blocks and blocks of uncared-for, subsidized houses trashed by those who take no responsibility for their domiciles. Sounds like that's also the future of your project. I thought you Americans cherished the concept of private property."

For a second, there's total silence. My older sister is glaring at that corner of the couch. If I know our Shar, she's a ticking bomb ready to go off in . . . Five. Four. Three. Two. I don't make it to one in my countdown before Shar jumps up. "*All* 'private property' in North America is stolen, right, Ms. Consuela? Every bit of Sunny Creek's land belonged to your people."

Ms. Consuela nods, arms folded across her chest. She's scowling.

"I commend your organization's 'noble experiment,'" the booming voice responds, but The Intruder's tone sounds like she definitely isn't praising them. "*My* research documents how poor people and communities thrive when given the most freedom from outside control. It sounds like your organization will be dictating quite a lot for these so-called beneficiaries. But please, continue your discussion."

Baba fixes his eyes on Shar and his head tips slightly in a Bengali "no." In response, Shar rolls her eyes, but doesn't launch into a rebuttal. Instead, she stalks over to join me at the door. "Aaargh!" she mutters under her breath. Good. At least she's with me when it comes to this . . . person. Sister solidarity again.

"You make a good point, Dr. Som," says Mr. Flemming, breaking this second, even more awkward silence. "Our goal, of course, is to empower our clients. Let's shift back to the immediate task at hand: making sure the Johnson property gets demolished and put on the market. We can't underestimate the Historical Society's bid for preservation. Older, entrenched citizens can be formidable opponents."

Shar raises her hand. "Full disclosure, Mr. Flemming, a member of my own family is working with the Historical Society, and she's far from old. Here she is—Pandita, meet everyone. Everyone, this is my little sister."

All heads swivel; all eyes goggle. My face feels as hot as a pakora right out of the oven. How could Shar pull me into the limelight like this? Our solidarity comes and goes like sunshine in November. No, wait. Like . . . oh, forget it, I'm too embarrassed to think of a better simile.

"Listen in all you want, Pandita!" Mr. Flemming calls from across the room. "Golden State Dwellings believes in transparency. Okay, let's get to work!"

People stand, stretch, and start gathering in smaller groups. Even though there's nobody left on the couch, Baba and his "colleague" are still squashed against each other. She's saying something that only he can hear, and he's nodding, looking right into her eyes.

Canoodling, for sure.

Revolting.

Time to make my escape.

I lug the box of Historical Society keepers to my room, take out a yellow pad of paper, and try to write something about the Johnson family. But it's hard to concentrate. I keep remembering Baba staring into The Intruder's eyes.

Ma's eyes were ten times more beautiful.

# TWENTY-SIX

EARLY THE NEXT MORNING, I review what I wrote for Ms. Maryann to read at this afternoon's Council meeting. It's . . . terrible. Sounds more like a school report than a story that can change people's minds and hearts. I haven't been able to make Aunty Lydia come alive the way she does in my imagination.

Suddenly, I think of the yellow envelopes in my drawer. Maybe reading her own written words would breathe life into my boring report. For a moment, I'm tempted again to open them.

But no.

I can't do that to Aunty Lydia.

If any of her children or grandchildren are still alive, they're the rightful readers of those letters, not me.

I pull out my poetry notebook instead. I wrote one about fog a few months ago, so it's probably time to work on it again. Poems sound so different after you take a break from them. You see images and words better once you give them a rest.

**Fog**

*She comes in silently, covering all,*
*Enveloping softly, like a shawl.*
*Gloomy, silent, shy, and gray,*
*Moving slowly, she comes at day.*
*Spooky, unearthly, ghostly, and white,*
*Treading softly, she comes at night.*

Way too many adverbs. I change "silently" to "silence," which means I have to change "silent" to "quiet." I also replace "moving slowly" with "rolling in," even though it's a bit of a cliché. There. Maybe I should read this to Mr. Marvin? He might be able to help me with the piece I'm writing for the Council meeting, too. The bottom-line truth, though, is . . . I've been feeling badly about our last interaction; I should try and make things right between us.

It's still too early to visit Orchard Manor. The morning sunshine is making the ripe apricots on the trees in Ashar Jaiga sparkle like golden jewels. Thanks to the hideous fence, I won't be able to bite into a juice-filled fruit that fits sweetly into the curve of my palm. Even worse, if the Historical Society doesn't sway the Council at the meeting this evening, those trees will be gone forever. Stolen by time, like all of the past.

I turn to a blank page in the notebook. For some reason, I'm thinking of a walk in the woods last Christmas when Baba, Shar, Indy, and I escaped the house and rented a cabin at Lake Tahoe. I start writing, taking my time to pick the right words as I remember the wintry scene.

### The Thief of Time

*Her scraggly arm is a silhouette against the winter sky,*
*The claw that scratches the empty air echoes her lonely sigh,*
*Gone is the warmth of green foliage that covers with sweet embrace,*
*She prays and pleads for blossoming buds to shelter her wounded face,*
*Her only answer is the callous snow that comes to bury her grief,*
*And slyly takes the warmth that is left like a cold and sneaky thief.*

The words pour out on the page as if the poem had been drafted somewhere deep inside me. I read it again; it's rough. Picking up my pen, I cross out "slyly" and replace it with "slowly," and then change "wounded" to "broken." After reading it once more, I change the words back. Because my heart feels *exactly* like a wounded tree in a winter. Like *that* tree. And that's *exactly* how time works—my enemy *will* slyly take away my memories. It still needs edits, though. I'll have to revise it again, after I give it a rest.

Writing a poem about time has made it fly. Mr. Marvin will be on the porch by now. I roll up my lousy version of Aunty Lydia's story, secure it with a rubber band, tuck it in my bag along with my poetry notebook, and head to Orchard Manor.

As usual on a Saturday morning, my friend is on the porch, rocking up a storm, but he doesn't wave as I approach. In fact, he doesn't see me at all; he's got a hand over his face. As I walk up the stairs slowly, Mr. Marvin looks up and brushes his sleeve across his eyes.

He clears his throat. "Glad to see you, kid."

Is he *crying*? *Again?* "You, too, Mr. Marvin."

Leo's mother comes out carrying a tray with two cups of milky tea, warm scones, a big bowl of clotted cream, and currant jam.

Mr. Marvin manages a smile. "Now this is civilized. I'm glad that cook listens to you, Alodia. He's usually so crabby. I don't know what kind of magic you use on that curmudgeon."

The same kind she uses on him, obviously. I help myself to a scone.

As soon as she's gone, Mr. Marvin turns to me.

"I was worried that . . . well, I feel badly about how grumpy I acted the last time you came, kid. I'm sorry. I've . . . I've been thinking about my mother a lot lately. And missing her. It's no excuse, but that's probably the reason why I've been so cranky. I wish I could remember her better!"

My heart softens like the clotted cream I'm slathering

on this scone. Guess it doesn't matter if you're thirteen or eighty-something, you never stop missing your mother. "Mr. Marvin . . . I think I'm forgetting mine, too."

He's quiet. And then: "The mind might forget but the heart doesn't."

I mull over what my friend just said. It's a good thought. We rock, munch, and sip.

After a while, I pull out my notebook. "Ready for another poem, Mr. Marvin?"

"Of course. I'd be honored."

He closes his eyes while I read "Fog."

"Pandita, that's your best one yet! I felt like I was standing right there on Treasure Island, watching the fog pour in through the Golden Gate."

I sit up straighter in my chair. It *did* sound good when I read it out loud. "I worked hard on it. Did anything sound off to you? And is 'rolling in' a cliché?"

"Read it again, will you?"

After I do, he rubs his chin. "'Rolling in' *is* a bit of a cliché. Maybe you can use a metaphor, like Carl Sandburg did in his poem about fog. I have it memorized if you want to hear it. My mother loved that poem."

"Okay."

He clears his throat and starts reciting. "'Fog,' by Carl Sandburg. 'The fog comes on little cat feet. It sits looking over harbor and city on silent haunches and then moves on.'"

I take the poem in. It's short. But I can see that catlike fog coming in and out. "You're right! I need a metaphor. Oh, wait, I already have a simile—'like a shawl.' I've got it! I'll say, 'rolling out' instead of 'rolling in,' because that's what you do with a rolled-up shawl!"

"Perfect! There's that knack with words!"

I can feel my confidence swelling. This is just what I needed. I slip the rubber band off my draft of Aunty Lydia's story and unroll it. "Maybe you can help me with some prose, too. I'm trying to change people's minds about saving the Johnson property at the Council meeting today. I'll need to touch their hearts, but I can't seem to do it with this speech. Could I read it to you?"

He stops rocking. "I told you—nobody around here cares about the past."

"But if you'd just listen—"

His mouth twists into a scowl as he interrupts me. "I hate to see you wasting your summer. Take it from me: Don't fight this! That property is done for!"

I came here for encouragement before the Council meeting, and I get this instead? Suddenly, everything I'm feeling is too much to handle—sadness, anger, despair. I jump to my feet and stuff my notebook and the yellow paper back in my bag. This time, *I'm* the one who leaves *him* with his mouth open.

# TWENTY-SEVEN

WHEN INDY DRIVES SHAR AND me to Town Hall,
I'm squished in the back of the twins' Bug with a bunch
of picket signs for Golden State Dwellings. I'm tempted
to try and smash their signs with my body weight, but
I don't. I've brought along my failed attempt at writing
down Aunty Lydia's story, even though I haven't looked
at it or changed a word since I walked out on Mr. Marvin.

The parking lot is jammed. Indy leaves Shar and her
signs near the front of Town Hall, and we find a spot in
the grocery store lot across the street. Just as Indy's locking the car, Baba pulls up in the Chevy with *her*. Wonderful. I'm still fuming inside at Mr. Marvin, anxious
about the outcome of this meeting, and now I have to
deal with seeing The Intruder again?

"Hello, girls," she says, after climbing out of the car.
"I can hardly wait to see the fun. American democracy in
action."

"Hello, Dr. Som," Indy says, and nudges me.

"Hello," I mutter.

Outside Town Hall, Shar and a few others are picketing, holding signs that read AFFORDABLE HOUSING NOW! and DEMOLITION FOR FAIR HOUSING! My sister steps out of rotation and greets us with a terse nod. She's holding a sign that reads GOLDEN STATE DWELLINGS FOR ALL!

Peeling away without a backward glance, I walk into Town Hall. Councilmember Mathews and four other members of the Town Council are sitting behind a raised table in front of the American flag. One is Mayor Walsh, according to the placard in front of him. Flanking him are two men, Councilmember McDermott and Councilmember Bailey. The fourth, of course, is Mr. Reed, Katrina's father. A clerk checks their microphones and fills their water glasses. I glare at the men. None of them knew Ma, or Aunty Lydia, but they're about to destroy the memories of both of them.

I spot Ms. Margaret in the auditorium, sandwiched by a couple of empty seats. Plopping into one of them, I pull out the rolled-up piece of yellow paper from my bag. It's not great, but maybe if Ms. Maryann reads it in her mesmerizing, read-aloud librarian voice, she'll transform it into something that convinces two more of our five town leaders to vote with Councilmember Mathews.

"Is Ms. Maryann on her way?" I ask Ms. Margaret.

"Not coming." Her curt answer hits me hard. "Too sick. Now *I'm* going to have to read our position statement. Can you believe it?"

"Will you read this essay, too?" I try to hand Ms. Margaret the roll of yellow paper, but she pushes it away.

"Absolutely not. I'm barely going to get through the position statement. I've been terrified of reading aloud since my school days."

"Couldn't Councilmember Mathews read the statement? And my essay?"

"She's a voting member of the Council. They only open the floor to the public."

Ugh! Why did Ms. Maryann have to get sick today of all days? *Now* who's going to read Aunty Lydia's story? Maybe Indy? I scurry back to where my sister is sitting with Lily, Tom, and a bunch of other high school theater people. Thankfully, she's at the end of the row, so I beg her in a low voice to read it, but she, too, shakes her head.

"I'd make a mess of it, Pundit," she whispers. "I don't know anything about that property. You do it. Just practice some of the things Ms. Harper's already taught you."

Scowling, I head back to my seat.

On the other side of the room, Katrina and Jemma are leaning against the wall. Leo's with them. He waves, and so does Jemma, and I reply with a quick palm lift. Katrina isn't looking my way, but that's nothing unusual. Wonder what her mom thinks of her spending so much time with two "newcomers" to Sunny Creek. At least Mrs. Reed wasn't able to make Katrina quit drama camp.

Along the back of the meeting room, black-suited men are lined up like crows waiting for scraps after a picnic.

"Who are those guys?" I ask Ms. Margaret.

"Developers," Ms. Margaret whispers back. "Ready to put offers on the table. If the demolition gets approved, prospective buyers will face a deadline to bid on the property. Sunny Creek's in for a zoning battle if the seller accepts an offer from that nonprofit or from a commercial office developer."

*The seller.* Who and where are Aunty Lydia's son or grandchildren, anyway? Why aren't they trying to save her legacy? Probably all they care about is money. I'd like to . . . give them a piece of my mind . . . too cliché . . . hurl a huge chunk of anger right at their selfish heads.

Mr. Reed leans over to say something to Mayor Walsh, who nods and turns on his microphone.

"Glad to see such a good turnout," the mayor says. "Tonight, your Council will vote on this question: Should the owner of the property, hereafter known as 'Johnson Family Trust,' be permitted to demolish the structures and orchard on fifteen acres of land bordered by Apricot and Strawberry Streets and Third and Fourth Avenues?"

It kills me that the mayor of our town sounds bored asking what feels like the most important question on my planet.

He drones on. "First, we'll hear environmental and agricultural reports, and then a statement submitted by the Preservation Society asking us to designate the buildings and orchard as town historical landmarks."

I try to follow the inspector's report about termite infestation and soil disease, but his language is too scientific. I get the picture, though, and so does everyone else in the room: Aunty Lydia's buildings and trees are in such bad shape they're not worth saving. This is exactly what the developers and Golden State Dwellings were hoping to hear.

The property inspector is winding down. "We recommend starting demo sooner rather than later, as the structures are in danger of collapsing."

No, they are NOT! Those stairs, maybe. But that porch supported Ma, our swing, and me perfectly! For years!

The mayor peers over his glasses at the agenda in front of him. "We will now hear from Margaret Gilbert, representing Sunny Creek's Historical Preservation Society."

As Ms. Margaret pushes past my knees, I can feel her legs trembling. She makes her way to the microphone, takes a deep breath, and starts reading. She was right—she's bad at this. She stumbles over every word that's longer than one syllable.

"It's our pro-pro-pose-proposal that the town should buy the pro-pert-property, restore it, and set up a park as well as a muse-museum to teach future gener-at-generations about local history . . ."

Nobody's paying attention to Ms. Margaret's jumpy

voice as she struggles to read the statement aloud. I hear rustling; people are starting to whisper. Mr. Reed is reading something hidden on his lap. Another councilmember is yawning. This is exactly what happens in the theater at drama camp when I speak.

Ms. Margaret forges on, hands shaking. "We're asking the town to inter-intervene and try to convince the owner to sell the parcel and struct-structures therein to Sunny Creek. Please vote to preserve this historically signif-significant property. Thank you."

As she collapses into the chair next to me, I feel the heat emanating from her body. Mopping her face and the back of her neck with a handkerchief, she mutters: "If Maryann's not on her deathbed, I'm going to put her there." All I can do is feel sorry for her. A lifetime of struggling to speak in public is terrible to imagine. That's me in fifty years, I think. Still scared wordless.

Katrina's father leans into his microphone. "Let's make this fast, shall we? As we all know, a decade ago, the town spent a significant sum of money to buy buildings and a parcel of land to set up our fine Heritage Museum and orchard. I'm not sure how different preserving this property would be from that. Anyway, I think we all know how this is going to go. I move that the Council approve the demolition."

"Second," says Councilmember McDermott.

"All in favor?" asks the mayor.

Councilmember Mathews leans into her mic. "Shouldn't we open this up to comments from the floor?"

"Of course, of course," Mayor Walsh says. "Forgot my Robert's Rules of Order for a quick minute. We have a motion on the table. Does anyone wish to speak before we vote? If so, please make your way forward."

There's a buzz in the room but nobody gets up. Panic is rising in my throat. This is when Ms. Maryann could have read Aunty Lydia's story in her likable, confident voice. She might have convinced them, even if what I've written isn't that good. Our whole town respects and knows her. But she's not here, and the yellow roll of paper is in my hand.

Mr. Reed scans the audience. "I'm sure we'd all like to enjoy the rest of this beautiful Saturday afternoon. So unless there's anyone else who wants to speak in defense of preserving this property, I think we should vote."

The crowd claps, and Mr. Reed flashes a middle-aged man's version of Katrina's smile.

I shove the yellow paper over to Ms. Margaret again, but she shakes her head violently and holds up both hands so she doesn't have to take it.

"All right, then, any councilmember in favor of demolition, please—"

I stand up.

My feet are carrying me to the front of the hall.

I'm at the microphone now.

170

"I'd like to speak."

My heart's pounding, my throat's as dry as stale naan, but I've said it.

Mayor Walsh leans into his microphone. "Young lady, did you say you'd like to speak to this issue?"

I nod. In the blur of faces staring at me, my family comes into focus. Baba's eyebrows are so high they've vanished into his curly hair. Indy's and Shar's mouths are open in identical circles.

The clerk lowers the microphone so it's at the right height for my face. When she's done, I clear my throat, take the rubber band off the yellow paper, and unroll it. I try desperately to remember what Ms. Harper taught me about engaging listeners and projecting my voice, but I can't think of anything besides taking deep breaths. Inhale. Exhale. Inhale. Exhale. And then start reading.

"One crisp autumn day in a place that was called the Valley of Heart's Delight, Lydia Johnson and her husband, Anders, bought a parcel of land next door to . . ." Oh, no! I can feel my voice slip into that super-low, super-flat mode. I clear my throat again and start over. "One crisp autumn day in a place—"

"I'm sorry, but we can't hear you!" Mr. Reed booms from the front.

"Turn the volume up, please," Councilmember Mathews says.

The clerk dashes over to the speakers and checks their volume. "It's on the highest setting."

"Kindly speak up, young lady," says Mayor Walsh.

"She is trying, sir!" Is that The Intruder?

"Give her a chance!" Wait . . . is that *Shar*?

"Please speak UP, young lady," an unknown voice calls out.

Once again, I start: "One crisp autumn day in a place that was called the Valley of Heart's Delight, Lydia Johnson and her husband, Anders . . ." My voice trails off. It's no use. I can barely hear myself. This isn't speaking; it's a low murmur that probably nobody but my mother could understand. And she's not here.

"You're finished, right, sweetie?" Mr. Reed asks, but it sounds more like a statement than a question. "Moving on, then . . ."

I stumble back to my seat. My throat is tight, my eyes are stinging. Ms. Margaret pats my hand.

"Time has destroyed that house and orchard," Mr. Reed is saying. I hate that his voice booms to the back of the room and out the door. "We've preserved the memories of our town in the Heritage Museum, but in this case, we can't let the past hinder the future. Let's vote, Bob."

"I think you're right, Frank," says Mayor Walsh. "All councilmembers in favor of the motion to approve demolition, please say 'aye.'"

Four hands go up, including the mayor's. "Aye."

"All opposed? Please say 'Nay.'"

*Nay, nay, nay!*

Councilmember Mathews shoots me a sympathetic look and raises her hand. "Nay."

"The vote stands: four to one, in favor of granting permission for demolition." The mayor cranes his neck to nod at someone in the back. "Your seller's crew can start work tomorrow. Council will start discussing zoning issues once a bid is accepted. This meeting is adjourned."

# TWENTY-EIGHT

WHEN I COME DOWNSTAIRS THE next morning, Indy's left a note by a plate of French toast. "Lily, Tom, and I are at the farmers market. Meeting Dr. Som and Baba near the fountain in the park for lunch. Come join us."

No, thanks. As if I'm going to enjoy a picnic after yesterday's disaster. I locked myself in my room last night as soon as we got home so my tears could flow without an audience. And who wants to spend more time with The Intruder? Not me.

Instead, I cross the street to Ashar Jaiga. In the spot where rosemary and oleander bushes used to hide our entrance, I press my eye against the mesh of the fence. This is my last glimpse of the roof of the house, the last birdsong in the orchard with small golden orbs glowing in the branches of its trees.

Mr. Marvin was right; trying to save the property was a lost cause.

Couldn't save it.

Goodbye, Place of Hope.

Goodbye, memories of Ma.

Suddenly, a hand rests on my shoulder and I turn. It's Jemma. Her cheeks are sunburned and she's still in church clothes—a crisply ironed, pleated yellow dress and wedge sandals like the ones Indy gave me for my birthday.

"I finally figured out why you wanted to save this orchard so badly," she says. "Yesterday, while you were talking, I remembered sneaking inside this property once with you and your mother."

"You did?" Because I can only picture Jemma and I being with Ma at our house, or at the park.

"We were about four, I think. We picked apricots and played ring-around-the-rosy. Your Ma sang songs in Bangla. It was so peaceful and fun."

As she's talking, a memory comes back, fuzzy but real. "It was." Tears fill my eyes. "It always was."

She's quiet for a bit, peering through the fence with me. Then: "Did you spend a lot of time here after . . . your mom was gone?"

"I did."

"So that's where you were when I couldn't find you? Here, by yourself?"

"Yep."

"I thought you were avoiding me. When I asked where you'd been, you'd change the subject. You were so secretive."

Her words sting a little—because she's right. I *was*

secretive. "Maybe it felt like that, but coming here wasn't something I could share. Ma asked me to keep it a secret."

Jemma doesn't respond.

"You thought *I* was avoiding *you*, and I thought *you* were done with *me*," I say. "I guess we were both wrong."

Jemma rests her forehead against the wire mesh and still doesn't say anything.

"Jemma?"

And then, without looking at me, she says, "I needed you, Pandita. My parents weren't talking, Appa was traveling back to Seoul all the time for work . . . and then he left for good last summer. Dumped Umma and me for some woman in Korea and *her* children."

Oh. Baba didn't tell me that part of it; all he'd said was that the Kims were divorcing. How hard to have your father choose another family over you and your mom! Poor Jemma! She'd stuck with me for two years after Ma died. Then she lost her father, in a different way. And I hadn't been there for her.

"I feel terrible, Jemma. I'm so, so sorry that you had to go through that without me."

Another silence. I sneak a look at Jemma's face. Tears are flowing down her cheeks now, so it's my turn to put a hand on her shoulder. After a bit, she reaches into her pocket, pulls out a tissue, and blows her nose. Then she manages to smile at me through her tears. "I was so glad when you showed up at drama camp! We didn't have any classes together last year, so I hardly saw you at school."

I lift my hand from her shoulder. "I was there. All year long. I saw you. But you were always with Katrina." There. It's out.

She doesn't seem surprised that I've brought up my replacement. "You don't know what it's like, being an only child, Pandita. You've always had your sisters around. Katrina's an only child, too, like me. Anyway, she was there when you didn't seem interested."

*Well,* that *sure seems upside down.* "I could never get alone time with you. I called! I came by your house, but your mom always said you were busy. After a while, I got the message and stopped trying."

"You were the one who was hard to find!" she says.

*Agree to disagree. That's what friends do sometimes.* "Well, I won't be hard to find now that this place is gone. You heard the mayor. Demolition starts tomorrow."

Jemma wipes the tears from her cheeks and looks back at the orchard. "I'm sorry you're losing your special place, Pandita. And I'm sorry that we . . . got messed up in our friendship. Can we . . . Do you think we can start over again?"

I've been waiting to hear those words for what feels like forever. "Yes, Jemma. I've been missing you so much."

We hug for the first time in months, and it feels like I'm one of the von Trapp children hugging Maria when she comes back. We hug for so long that we start giggling and can't stop. By the time we finish laughing and hugging, my stomach muscles ache. In a good way.

Then a shadow of concern flashes across Jemma's face. "Won't you give Katrina a chance, Pandita? She's really a loyal friend."

Ugh, why? After last night's vote, I want nothing to do with the Reeds! Besides, now that Jemma and I are back together, why does she need Katrina? But there's so much hope in her voice. "I'll try," I say.

Jemma beams. "I'm heading to the farmers market now to meet her. Leo's going to be there, too. We had such a good time yesterday on the boat. I wish you'd been with us. Want to come with me now? It'll take your mind off . . . tomorrow."

I take one last, long look at Ashar Jaiga. Operation Remember Ma might be failing, but Operation Win Back Jemma seems to be revving up. So I nod. "Okay, sure. That sounds fun."

"Hooray!" Jemma throws her arms around me in another tight squeeze, and I can't help it. I start giggling all over again.

We walk past the school, Orchard Manor, and the library, laughing and talking just like the old days. This feels so right, I almost forget the humiliation of last night. As we meander through the park and the playground, I remember how we spent hours pushing each other on the swings. The two of us have a good history. You don't just throw that away forever.

But then, suddenly, my canvas shoes turn into stones.

A couple is strolling on the path in front of us.

They stop.

I know Jemma sees them, too, because I hear the quick intake of her breath.

The woman turns to the man and reaches up with both palms. She's a lot shorter than he is, so she has to stand on tiptoe to pull his face close to hers.

She kisses him.

I wait for him to pull away, but, to my horror, he bends even more, and their kiss goes on and on as if he's been waiting for this moment for years.

Which he has.

Because he's my Baba.

And that's not Ma he's kissing.

# TWENTY-NINE

I WAKE UP EARLY THE next morning with my stomach growling. I haven't eaten anything since yesterday morning. After Jemma and I saw Baba and Dr. Som (yuck), I couldn't bring myself to go to the farmers market. Jemma hid with me behind a tree until they passed, then held my hand as she walked me home. I was grateful she didn't ask questions.

I braid my hair and gaze at the sad-faced girl in the mirror. There's something I need to do today before the demolition begins.

Downstairs, Shar and Indy are eating breakfast. Baba's nowhere in sight.

"Why didn't you join us yesterday?" Indy asks as soon as she sees me.

I don't answer. I just shrug and help myself to a bowl of cereal.

Shar groans. "I needed you, Pundit; Indy made me join them for lunch and I had to sit through another lecture. That woman thinks she's an expert on the American housing crisis and she's only been here a month."

"Give Dr. Som a chance, Shar." Indy turns back to me. "And you, too. Okay, I'll ask it again: Why didn't you come, Pundit? I left a note."

I set my cereal spoon down harder than I mean to. "I *did* come. I was on my way, but then I saw . . ." It's hard to say it, but I don't want to be the only one holding this. "I saw Baba with . . . HER, and . . . she . . . kissed him."

Complete silence. Shar's stopped chewing mid-bite.

"Did he kiss her back?" Indy asks.

I nod.

Shar swallows.

Indy takes a swig of orange juice.

Then my sisters start talking at the same time.

"Bengali couples don't kiss in public." That's Indy.

"Ma and Baba never kissed in public," Shar says.

"This person doesn't seem too traditional to me," I say. "She definitely made the first move."

Another silence. Shar's head is down. After a bit, Indy gives herself a little shake. "What a whirlwind romance! I told you Baba was a catch. Shar? You okay?"

"It's . . . kind of a shock," Shar says, her face still buried in her arms. Her usually strong, confident voice sounds muffled and shaky.

Part of me is glad that she seems as devastated as I

feel. Another part feels guilty for bringing it up. Maybe it's time to change the subject. "At least Jemma and I are friends again. We were going to the farmers market together before we ran into Baba."

It works. Shar looks up.

"Oh, that's wonderful, Pundit!" Indy says.

"And drama camp gets the credit, right?" Shar's voice is starting to steady again.

I shrug. "Some of it, maybe. But she reached out to me thanks to that awful Council meeting, actually. I was so embarrassed! I bombed so badly."

"I'm proud of you for giving it a try," Shar says.

"Even though I was working against you?"

"Even so."

"I couldn't believe you were up there!" Indy adds.

"Again, drama camp," Shar says. Weirdly, I'm glad that she sounds so smug. "Keep listening to Ms. Harper. Next time you speak at a town meeting, your voice will be ready."

There won't be a next time, but I don't want an argument. I shovel down my cereal and start rummaging through kitchen drawers until I find scissors and ribbon.

It's still early when I head out the front door. A loud chorus of different birds are welcoming the morning sun, both here and across the street. No machines yet, but they'll be here soon. The roses and hydrangea bushes Ma planted by the front porch are flowering, so I clip some blooms and tie the stems together with the ribbon. Then, carrying my makeshift bouquet, I walk until the birdsong from Ashar Jaiga fades away behind me.

It's not far to the Lutheran church, and the gate to the small cemetery next to the church is open. Thankfully, nobody's here to be curious about an unknown Indian kid being here, so I wander the rows of graves, reading headstones until I find it.

ANDERS JOHNSON

BORN MAY 18, 1881, STOCKHOLM, SWEDEN

DIED APRIL 18, 1906, SUNNY CREEK, CALIFORNIA

JAG ÄR UPPSTÅNDELSEN OCH LIVET

I AM THE RESURRECTION AND THE LIFE

I place the flowers at the bottom of the headstone.
There.
This feels right.

And then I stand with my head bowed for a bit, thinking of Mr. Johnson. *Uncle Anders*, that is. And Aunty Lydia. And then, for a long while, of my mother.

I check my watch as I leave the cemetery. I have time before drama camp to stop by the library. Ms. Maryann and I are good enough friends to speak truthfully. How could she not have shown up at the meeting?

The library just opened, so it's as quiet as a . . . tomb, no, that's too stale . . . as an empty refrigerator. There, that's better, because the air-conditioning hum sounds like a fridge. I march into the children's room, ready to interrogate Ms. Maryann. But as soon as I see her at her desk, nose still red from her cold, my frustration dwindles. She looks . . . shattered.

"Oh, Pandita! I'm so sorry I let you down. I'm feeling well enough to work today, but on Saturday morning I had a one-hundred-and-three-degree fever and couldn't get myself out of bed no matter how hard I tried. Margaret told me how you got up to speak. Thank you for trying."

"You didn't see me up there. I'm sure the rest of the town thinks I'm an idiot."

"People with sense in their heads know it took courage to try."

I feel slightly better. "But I couldn't even make it past the first sentence, Ms. Maryann."

"Knowing your love of words, I'm sure it was a humdinger. In fact, I'd like to read all that you wrote about the Johnsons, if you ever want to share it."

I think about the piece of yellow paper that's locked in my drawer along with Aunty Lydia's letters. "Maybe one day, Ms. Maryann. For now, I don't want to think about that property anymore."

"I understand," Ms. Maryann says. "Oh! I have *Anne of Green Gables* back in stock. That should cheer you up!"

"Actually, do you have any *new* books to recommend?"

Her eyebrows go up. "New books? I don't think I've

ever heard you ask for those. But yes, of course I do." She gets up and comes back with two. "Try *Roll of Thunder, Hear My Cry* by Mildred D. Taylor, and *Dragonwings* by Laurence Yep. I can't wait to hear what you think. Yep's book is about a Chinese boy who immigrates to San Francisco. He wrote a whole series that starts with this one. It might help you process what's happening in Sunny Creek right now."

As I tuck the books into my bag, Leo, Jemma, and Katrina walk into the library. Leo looks a shade darker, and Katrina's cheeks are sunburned, just like Jemma's. From the boat ride, probably. A quick wave of that old left-out feeling washes away as Jemma smiles warmly at me. I still can't believe we're friends again. But then she gives me a "you promised" kind of look and tips her head in Katrina's direction.

Oh, yeah. I did say I'd try, didn't I? "Hey, Katrina. Hey, Leo."

"I'm so glad you're here, Pandita," Leo says. "I couldn't wait to tell you how brave you were to get up in front of everyone like that."

Jemma throws Katrina a "your turn" look. "Uh, yeah, you were brave," Katrina says.

"Er . . . thanks," I say, trying to ignore Ms. Maryann's "I told you so" expression.

"I'm glad you're here, too, Ms. Maryann," says Leo, "because I have something I want to tell you *and* Pandita."

Ms. Maryann and I exchange a curious glance.

"I'd like to invite you both to my first concert in Sunny Creek," Leo says.

"Concert?" Ms. Maryann asks. "That's great, Leo. Where will it be?"

"At that fancy Italian restaurant in town," says Jemma.

"My mother had me play and sing for the owner, and they called to ask me to perform," says Leo. "I sang the Emily Dickinson poem you shared with me, Ms. Maryann, so it's really thanks to you that I got the gig. It's a week from Friday."

She takes a little curtsy. "I accept the invitation. The credit is all yours, young troubadour."

"That's wonderful, Leo!" I say. But I can't help wishing I'd been the first friend he'd told.

"It's not a real concert, only background music while people eat," Leo says. "Mostly music only; no words. If only I could write like Emily Dickinson! It's easy to compose music, but I'm terrible at lyrics."

Ms. Maryann glances around. The children's section is empty except for the four of us. "Play one with just music for us now, Leo. Maybe the girls and I can think of another poem that might fit."

Right away, Leo says, "I'd love to. I always hear mistakes better when I play for other people. Okay with you to hear a work in progress?"

"It's definitely okay." Katrina answers for all of us.

He's so ready to play something that isn't finished! Meanwhile I can't share a poem until it's close to perfect. And even then, I'll only read it to Mr. Marvin. Or I used to, before we started getting mad at each other.

Leo opens his case and pulls out his guitar. He slings the strap around his neck, twangs a string, listens, and adjusts the pegs on the end of the guitar's neck. And then he starts playing a cheerful, old-fashioned-sounding tune that somehow reminds me of rain. Birch trees moving in the wind. Animals scurrying around. As I keep listening, I realize I'm thinking of my poem, "Rain in the Forest." It was the one that made Mr. Marvin smell rain on a sunny day.

The song ends, and as we applaud, Leo puts down his guitar and takes a bow.

"People are going to love listening to that kind of music while they dine," Ms. Maryann says. "You really create a mood. That song reminded me of rain."

I can't believe it. "You thought of rain, too? I wrote a poem about rain once—" I catch sight of Katrina's face and stop talking. What am I doing? I never talk about my poems.

"You used to write poems when we were little," Jemma says. "But you never let me read them."

"She hasn't let me read them, either," Ms. Maryann says. "Even when I've begged. I gave up asking a while ago."

"I almost got to hear one the other day," says Leo.

My cheeks are so hot, I wonder for a moment if they're sunburned, too.

"Something about this feels right," Ms. Maryann says. "Leo's music and Pandita's poems? I'd love to hear that combination. I'll definitely be at your concert, Leo. I can't wait."

Katrina glances at her watch. "Camp in ten minutes, people."

Leo walks beside me as we head out the door. "Does time go fast when you're writing poems?"

"It flies," I say. "I forget all about tracking it sometimes, in fact. Trying to find the right word or phrase is so interesting."

"Same thing happens when I'm trying to find the right chord or note. Ms. Maryann's idea isn't bad. Would you share that poem about rain with me? Maybe I *could* set it to my music."

He averts his eyes as he waits for my answer, as if he knows it's a Big Ask. And it is. But then I think of how he came to help me in the town meeting hall just when I needed it. I remember how he respected Aunty Lydia's privacy, and mine, when he found the yellow envelopes. And the way he sings! His voice makes my insides feel like . . . one of Indy's warm and mushy sugar cookies, fresh out of the oven. Suddenly, there's nothing I'd like more than to hear one of my poems sung in that voice.

"Let's give it a try," I say.

"Great! Can I come to your house this afternoon?"

"Sure, but . . ." Oops. I need to get my sisters ready for Leo's visit. I haven't had a friend over since Jemma, and I've *never* had a visitor who's a boy. "Um, Leo . . . can you give me about an hour after camp before you come?"

"Okay. I'll hang out at Orchard Manor."

"Come through the side gate to the kitchen door. Our front porch is a mess."

"Will do. And shoes off inside, right?"

"Right." It's nice not having to explain that custom.

# THIRTY

BEFORE WE GET UNDERWAY FOR the day, Ms. Harper and Mr. Jackson both take the time to come to where I'm sitting and commend me for getting up to the microphone at the Council meeting. So do Lily and Tom. I'd seen Indy's theater friends sitting with her, but I hadn't realized both teachers were there, too.

I thank them, but I don't believe them. How did it feel seeing one of their actors fail miserably in front of so many people? I wonder if they're secretly regretting the decision to give me a speaking role. I certainly would be.

"Maybe I can *sing* the lines?" I ask Ms. Harper after another failed attempt at acting later that morning. "Leo might be able set them to music for me."

"No, but you can try saying them with the same resonance and inflection that you do when you sing. Let's take it from the top, Pandita."

I catch the rolling-eye exchange between a couple of members on Team Hollywood. I would be annoyed with me, too. Will I single-handedly wreck the entire production? I picture Mrs. Reed's "I told you so" expression in the auditorium as I freeze up during our performance. I can't let that happen. I'm not giving up. Not yet, anyway.

I breathe a sigh of relief later as Team Hollywood walks to the cafeteria for Ms. Lee's dancing session. This, I can handle.

Our dance teacher reviews her instructions for the box step and has us practice on our own for a bit. Then, while Tom starts playing "My Favorite Things" on the boom box, Ms. Lee calls Joey and Katrina forward to give us an example of waltzing together. Joey's somewhat shorter than Katrina, but that doesn't seem to matter— the two of them twirl around the room like they're at an Austrian ball. We clap when they're done.

"I've been practicing with my grandma," Joey says, bowing.

"Me, too!" says Katrina.

It's time for the rest of us to partner up. Jenny and I give it a whirl, with me leading while she follows. We're pretty good—not as good as Joey and Katrina, but almost. My braids swing around as if they're waltzing, too. I catch sight of Jemma and Leo stumbling over each other's feet. Ms. Lee walks over to them and tells the rest of us to switch partners. I turn to the girl playing Sister Berthe, who starts shoving and yanking my waist like she's trying to wrestle me instead of lead me in the waltz.

"Here; you follow, I'll lead," I say. We switch, and soon she's smiling as we one-two-three gracefully around the room. This is fun. We even start singing along: "Girls in white dresses with blue satin sashes . . ."

"Pandita, come here!" Ms. Lee calls. "Tom, stop playing, please!"

Leaving my partner waltzing around the room by herself without music, I walk to Leo and Jemma, who both look miserable.

"Can you dance with Leo, Pandita?" Ms. Lee asks. "Jemma, watch how her feet move, will you?"

My heart starts beating a one-two-three. Leo places his right hand on my waist. I drop my left hand on his shoulder, and our eyes meet. So do our other hands. And then Leo smiles; his whole face relaxes.

"Let's go, Pandita," he says.

Ms. Lee starts with a slow count, and my feet move backward in a box step. Leo's hand on my waist isn't doing much to guide me, so I use mine on his shoulder to pull him gently forward and back. Soon, we're dancing more fluidly, so Ms. Lee asks Tom to restart the music.

"Raindrops on roses and whiskers on kittens . . ."

We're waltzing. One, two, three, and a zing and a flutter.

Leo-von Trapp and Pandita-Maria.

"And then I don't feeeeeeel so baaaaad," Leo sings in my ear.

When Ms. Lee asks Tom to stop the music, Leo and I let each other go at exactly the same moment.

"Your turn, Jemma," I say, and she steps forward.

Ms. Lee starts her slow count again. This time, Leo moves more confidently, and the two of them are able to execute a few box steps.

"Thanks, Pandita," Jemma calls over Leo's shoulder as they waltz away.

At least one of my birthday goals didn't crash and burn. It's so, so good to have our old friendship back, even with Katrina around. And Leo . . . well, that's something new, but getting better by the day.

# THIRTY-ONE

IT'S A GOOD THING I'M finally having fun at drama camp, because the demolition across the street is miserable. Machines of destruction are whining, grinding, and crunching by the time I get home. It feels like they're ripping up my insides; I can't even look over there to see if the house is still up.

Inside the kitchen, Indy's experimenting with a recipe—smells like chocolate cake—and Shar's reading a report. It seems like they've been home more lately this summer—or maybe it's that I've lost my escape—but I don't really want them around today.

"I have a friend coming over," I say, joining Shar at the table. May as well get their questioning over with sooner rather than later.

Shar looks up from her report. "Jemma?"

"Nope. Although she'll be coming over  soon, I'm sure. Just not today." Somehow, though, I can't picture Katrina in our house. But maybe.

"So . . . who's coming over today, then?" Indy asks.

"His name's Leo."

Shar and Indy exchange an irritating glance.

"Is that the kid Lily's been raving about?" Indy asks. "The one who sings like he could already be on Broadway? Do tell!"

"Yes. He's playing Captain von Trapp."

But if I were writing a note to Ma—which I haven't done since my birthday—I'd have to be totally honest and add, *He's a boy, Ma, and I'm not sure why but my stomach sways a little bit when I'm near him. And when he put his hand on my waist while we waltzed, it felt like my heart was . . . drinking a delicious cup of tea.*

"He and his family just moved to town," I say. "His mom is a nurse at Orchard Manor, and she asked me to be his friend since he's new. Don't get strange about him being a boy, okay, you two?"

Silent twin-talk ensues. I wait.

"We won't, Pundit," Shar says. "Most of my friends are boys, so you don't have to worry about me saying something awkward."

"Or me," Indy adds. "This is strictly you being kind to someone new to town."

I throw her a suspicious look. "Indy, he's a FRIEND."

"I get it, I get it. I'll be good, I promise."

I go up to my room to wait for Leo and close the window to drown out the noise from across the street. I started *Roll of Thunder, Hear My Cry* in the auditorium when I was waiting for my scenes and I've already torn through a hundred pages. I love the rhythm of Ms. Taylor's words in the descriptive parts. The title itself reads like a poem. One part jumps out now: *"How you carry yourself, what you stand for—that's how you gain respect. But, little one, ain't nobody's respect worth more than your own."*

Maybe Shar was right—I would respect myself less if I hadn't at least given it a try at the Council meeting. I read until the doorbell rings and then race downstairs so nobody else can open the door.

Leo's brought along some leftover scones from Orchard Manor. I show him into the kitchen, where my sisters are perched like twin vultures.

"Leo, Indy and Shar. Shar and Indy, Leo," I say, getting a plate for the scones.

"Indy? Is that short for India?" He puts his guitar case down by the kitchen table.

Indy jumps up to take her chocolate cake out of the oven. "Nope. I'm named after Indira Gandhi, the first female prime minister of India. And Shar is named after the Bengali movie star Sharmila Tagore."

"Our parents got it backward," Shar tells him. "I'm the political one, and Indy loves the stage and screen. But Pandita's named after a woman who used to care for widows, Pandita Ramabai. Which is perfect, because our Pandita is good with old people, too."

Ugh. Not anymore. I feel a pang for Mr. Marvin. I

haven't seen him since I left in such a huff. Does he miss me, I wonder?

Indy reaches for a scone and takes a bite. "Oh, my, these are good."

Leo perches on a stool. "Aren't they? It's my mother's recipe. But that cake looks and smells incredible."

Indy smiles as she cuts the cake. "I like your friend, Pundit."

"Pundit?" echoes Leo.

My cheeks blaze up. "That's what the twins call me."

"Pundit means 'wise one,'" Shar explains. "That's what they called the other Pandita, too. Besides, Pandita's always been sort of timeless and mystical, with her poetry and quiet presence."

She's making me sound like a mountaintop guru in saffron-colored robes. I try to send her a nonverbal to *zip it*.

"My mother noticed that, too," Leo says, as Indy hands him a wedge of cake. He takes a big bite. "Oh, wow." After he swallows, he imitates his mother's voice: "'She's an old-fashioned girl who values old things and old people.'"

My sisters laugh. "Smart woman," Indy says.

Time to correct these skewed impressions of Pandita Paul. "I've decided to try new things. Like books, for example. I started one today that I've never read before." Both Indy and Shar are shocked into silence. I decide to use this as an exit cue. "Leo, we better get started. We only have an hour before your mom comes to pick you up."

"We could drive you home," Indy offers. "Where do you live, anyway?"

"No, it's okay," he says. "Orchard Manor's nearby, so it's easy for her to get me. We live in that tall building by the mall. We just moved there a month ago."

"You got one of *those* apartments?" Shar asks. "I heard there was a long waiting list."

"Yeah. The owner gave us priority because his father lives at Orchard Manor." He grins at me. "Pandita's going to have to come over soon and try my parents' cooking."

I can't help smiling back. That sounds so nice.

Indy gives me a significant glance. Uh-oh, she's getting weird. I put our empty cake plates in the sink. "Let's go into the living room, Leo."

"Thanks for the absolutely perfect-in-every-way slice of cake," he says, making Indy glow.

In the living room, Leo unpacks his guitar while I run upstairs to get my poetry notebook. Here we go. This is the first time I'll share a poem with someone who isn't Mr. Marvin.

This feels like . . . like handing over a map that leads to buried treasure, but I give Leo the notebook. It's already open to my poem about rain. Placing it on the coffee table in front of himself, he starts strumming the now-familiar melody. And then—he's taking the words *I* wrote and singing them along with *his* tune. Singing *my* poem. Song, I mean, because that's what it's becoming as he matches each line of my words to a line of music.

*It's raining in the forest*
*The wind is fresh and free*
*Squirrels running here and there*
*Trees bending in wild glee*
*The birds are so excited*
*And gladness fills the air*
*The brook turns to a fury*
*But no one seems to care*
*Sweet-smelling rain caresses*
*The flowers and the plants*
*And all the forest sways in tune*
*To the wind's inviting dance*

As I sit back on the couch and listen, it feels like the rainy, windy music is clearing out the muck in my heart.

"What do you think, Pandita?" he asks, after singing it a few times through. "Could I play it at my concert? And introduce you as the person who wrote the lyrics?"

Why not share the credit? "I'd like that." And then, hearing my own voice get softer and quieter, I ask Leo to play my—our—song one more time.

# THIRTY-TWO

ACROSS THE STREET. MACHINES GRIND on. I let myself look at the property only when they're finally done with demolition. What used to be Ashar Jaiga is now a big, flat, dusty piece of nothing, surrounded by a high fence and FOR SALE signs. A few apricot trees survived around the edge facing our house, but everything else is gone: orchard, garden, house, porch, swing, memories of Ma. The sight lands like a . . . punch in my gut . . . no . . . like a coffin at the bottom of a grave. Yes, that's better, but so, so hard to feel.

Baba's started bringing The Intruder home for supper almost every evening when they don't go out on a date. Indy's her usual welcoming self, and even Shar gets drawn into the conversation—through an argument, usually. Meanwhile, I sit, silent and stone-faced. I hate the way she flings her head back in a loud guffaw that resounds through the whole house. And wow, can she talk. Nonstop. Baba adored Ma. How in the world can he be attracted to her opposite?

Tonight, she and Shar have another heated discussion.

"You think *America* is prejudiced?" The Intruder asks. "Come to India and see our caste system. The lowest caste is stuck in poverty and servitude for generations. They clean bathrooms and sweep streets, and so do their children. But here, I see people with dark skin in all kinds of jobs and income brackets."

"Not too many when it comes to the best-paying ones," Shar retorts. "Most people in power in this country are white. And they want to hold on to it. Immigrants don't have as many opportunities as Americans born here do."

"If that were true, nobody would want to come," The Intruder says. "But everyone does. America is still the 'Land of Opportunity' for people in other countries, especially those who are persecuted or oppressed. We don't see long visa lines outside the Russian embassy or the Chinese embassy. You take your freedom and opportunity for granted."

That makes Shar furious, judging by her scowl. "I do not! I'm using it to make this country a better, more just place. That's what freedom is for—to serve others, not ourselves! But maybe that's not one of your values?"

Baba's shifting around in his armchair. He stands up. "Er . . . Shef, do you want to go for a walk?"

The Intruder stands. "I wouldn't mind, but I'm greatly enjoying this discussion, Anand. Talking with this daughter of yours is quite stimulating." She turns to Shar again.

"I'd like to hear how the planning is progressing for your voluntary organization's initiative when I return. I may have some new opinions to offer."

The door closes behind them. "I'm sure she has *lots* more opinions," Shar says.

Indy plops down in the armchair that The Intruder vacated. "Well, what's that old saying? 'Iron sharpens iron.' Maybe arguing with someone like that can help make your case stronger."

"She's even coming with us to Leo's concert on Friday," Shar says, ignoring Indy's positivity. "I think Baba's hoping we'll get used to having her around. It's a good thing we love him so much." With that, she stalks off to get ready for another meeting.

I settle down on the couch with a big sigh.

"Sigh all you want, Pundit, but the fact is that Baba enjoys Dr. Som's company," Indy says. "It was definitely time for him to start dating again. Think of how lonely Captain von Trapp was in *The Sound of Music*."

If only The Intruder were anything like Maria.

On the Thursday afternoon before Leo's concert, I run through my lines again and again in my room. I can manage them when I'm alone with Ms. Harper, but onstage, in front of my campmates, my voice still goes into hibernation. Ms. Harper keeps saying to be patient and focus on the exercises she's taught me, but it feels like we're hurtling toward our performance. Like I'm running out of time.

The phone rings in the kitchen. I run downstairs to pick it up, expecting it to be for Indy or Shar, but instead it's for me. It's Leo. We just said goodbye at camp an hour ago, but this is still a nice surprise. I sit on my favorite stool to talk, glad my family's not home yet.

"Tatay's been looking at rentals in San Jose," Leo says. *Tatay* is what he calls his Baba. "He thinks we can afford to rent a whole house there."

"Are you moving?" For some reason, the thought makes my stomach flip.

"Not if Nanay has her way. Their arguments are sure heating up, though. She's making me wear an ancient bow tie tomorrow at the restaurant, and I don't like to fight her when she gets fierce."

I'm winding the telephone cord around my finger and then freeing it again. "Sounds fancy."

"Wait till you see it. My Lolo used to wear that thing when he performed in the opera."

"Oh, that's nice. He gave you his talent. Why not take his tie, too?"

"Ha! Good point. Hey, when I introduce our song, you might want to stand up and take a bow."

Hmmmm . . . has he figured out I'll say "yes" to almost anything he'll ask? That's not good. I can hear

Shar's voice lecturing me in my head about women's rights. "Let me think about it."

"Sounds good. I hope people enjoy the music. This is my first real gig."

"You're going to be great!"

"Thanks, Pandita."

We talk about camp for a while and he asks a few questions about school. Eventually Leo's mom calls him for dinner and we hang up.

Putting the receiver back in the cradle, I go and flip through my poetry notebook. I started a poem a while back that I want to read again.

**Bold Beauty**
*The fountain erupts her silver song*
*The sun dazzles her shining hair*
*Misty rainbows arch their backs*
*Bowing to this maiden fair*

That's all I wrote, but it brings back a memory of watching the fountain in the park. I remember thinking that the sparkling arcs of water didn't care about my mesmerized eyes; they were too busy enjoying being themselves. That's what made them so . . . beautiful.

Suddenly, I close the notebook and get up. Standing in front of the mirror, my eyes travel down my body. I've grown a couple of inches this summer and my overalls are a bit too short. My white shirt feels tight, too. Outgrown overalls and a T-shirt probably aren't the best choice for my debut as a songwriter. Especially not with Leo wearing his grandfather's special bow tie.

Pushing through my hangers in my closet, I find the present Indy gave me on my birthday. I take off my overalls and zip myself into the dress. It fits perfectly. The strappy sandals do, too. Standing in front of the mirror, I twirl. The flowers in the folds of the golden material become a moving circle of color around my legs. *Like a portable meadow*, I think. Ooh, good title for a poem—"Portable Meadow."

Unbraiding my hair, I comb it out. It's long and thick, reaching to the middle of my back. Maybe I'll wear it loose for once.

I take stock again of the girl in the mirror. Now she looks ready to be introduced to an audience. She even looks ready for eighth grade. Seems like she's enjoying being herself, I think. Twirling again, I spot the hat Mr. Marvin gave me as a birthday present sitting on the closet shelf. I'll probably never wear that thing again; the sight of it just makes me sad about our broken friendship. I should stash it in the garage with the other giveaways.

I'm not used to heels, so I walk carefully down the stairs to the garage, carrying the hat. It takes a while to push through the unwanted junk that my sisters and Baba have piled in here. Finally, I find a box marked GIVEAWAYS, open it, and stuff the hat inside. As I put that box back, I see another one labeled ASHA. KEEPERS. PRIVATE. in Baba's handwriting. It's taped shut. Okay, Baba. I won't open it. But I'll bet this is where he found that Emily Dickinson book he gave me for my birthday.

Another box is beside it. This one isn't taped shut, though, and Baba's labeled it ASHA. CLOTHES. FOR THE GIRLS. Before I can think twice, I open it.

Even in the dim light filtering through the high windows along the garage wall, I recognize the outfit on top. It's a green-and-white shalwar chameez that our mother used to wear to Bengali parties. I finger the soft, silky material and immediately picture Ma coming down the stairs wearing this outfit. I savor the memory—the graceful movements, kind smile, and sweet voice greeting me as I looked up from the entry—like one of the delicious lunches she used to send with me to school.

After a while, I pull the tunic top out and hold it up against myself; it's almost the perfect length. There's a matching pair of pants under the tunic, and a scarf, too, that she'd drape around her neck and shoulders. I want to try the whole outfit on one day.

But not now, not today.

Today is for my new dress.

Folding Ma's shalwar carefully, I put it back in the box.

It's enough to know it's here, along with the memory.

# THIRTY-THREE

SHAR AND BABA ARE IN the kitchen watching Indy mix up a marinade for tandoori chicken, but they're not alone. The Intruder is here *again*. I thought I'd get a break from her presence until tomorrow at the concert. But no. She's perched on my favorite stool, and as my sister adds ingredients, she's describing Indy's movements like a sports commentator in that booming voice of hers.

*Why do certain people occupy so much space?* I think. Nobody's noticed me walking in wearing my new dress and wedge-heeled shoes. Pandita Paul, Invisible Girl, and in my own kitchen at that.

"Lovely dress." Great. She's the first to see me.

Shar jumps to her feet. "Wow, Pundit, you look . . . well, that dress is just right on you. Good job, Indy."

Indy spins around. "Oh, yes. You look . . . taller, and . . . I like your hair down like that."

"I'm dazzled," Baba says, pretending to rub his eyes. "Did a sunlit garden just walk in? No, no, that's my Pandu."

The Intruder is inspecting my dress with interested eyes. "Lovely material. You don't know this, Anand, but one of my hidden talents is sewing. I could probably replicate that dress you're wearing, Pandu."

I hear myself give a little gasp. I can't help it. She's used the nickname that only Ma, Baba, and my grandparents call me. Indy shoots me a look, but The Intruder doesn't seem to have noticed my reaction.

"Western clothes are fine, but they aren't as lovely as a shalwar chameez," she's saying, gesturing at the sparkly sapphire blue one she's wearing. "Have you girls ever tried on one of these? They're quite comfortable."

"Not since we were in . . ." Shar's voice trails off.

"No, not lately," Indy answers.

"Bring me a tape measure, will you, Anand? I'll take the girls' measurements right now and sew you up each a shalwar chameez. I'm quite fast, too. What colors do you prefer?"

What kind of timing is this? I just put away my mother's shalwar chameez, and now this woman wants to make me one? Too soon. Too much.

Baba clears his throat.

"That would be nice," Indy says. "Yellow."

Shar forces a smile. "Light blue."

I can't answer. There's a long, long pause. Indy shoots me a "for Baba's sake" look with her eyes. "Pink," I mutter.

Baba finds a tape measure. "This is so lovely and

generous of you, Shef," he gushes. As if she's offered to pay for our college educations.

One by one, The Intruder takes the three of us into the bathroom. Shar goes first, and then Indy. When it's my turn, I have to stand with arms stretched out while she measures every part of me and jots numbers on a piece of paper. My waist. Arms. Legs. Hips. Even my chest.

"You are starting to bloom," she tells me. "I'll add extra material to that area in case you fill out even more."

I don't answer. I'm clenching my jaw and counting down the seconds of this mortification.

"Are you wearing that dress to Leo's concert?" Indy asks when I'm finally released into the kitchen. "Guess I'll get dressed up, too."

"I reserved a table for five," Baba says. "Shef, I'm so glad you're joining us."

"I am also, Anand."

And then she stands on tiptoe to give Baba's cheek a kiss.

In front of his daughters.

How forward.

How un-Bengali.

Plus, the two of them are way too close to the potatoes and peas Indy's sautéing in the frying pan. I'm not eating a bite of aloo-mattar tonight, even though it's one of my favorites.

# THIRTY-FOUR

ON THE WAY TO THE restaurant the next night, I sit between the twins in the Chevy. It's been a long time since the three of us were back here together. We stay quiet, listening to the conversation and laughter in the front seat. I haven't said anything about Leo singing my poem. I might have if I could have had some time alone with Baba and my sisters, but The Intruder's been ever present. And now she's taken Ma's seat in the family car.

Our table is near the front of the restaurant, where Leo is setting up his microphone. He comes over and introduces himself to Baba and The Intruder. "Thanks for coming. I hope you enjoy the concert."

He doesn't look the least bit nervous. Meanwhile, my stomach is doing cartwheels. I have to keep arranging my hair back over my shoulders. Braids always kept it in place; now it's floating around like it has a mind of its own.

"You look nice, Pandita," Leo says. "See you after, okay? I want you to meet my Tatay."

The eyebrow-raise and smile from Indy are so irritating that I plop into my seat and look elsewhere. Jemma and Katrina are at a table with Mrs. Kim on the other side of the room. They're wearing dresses, too. Wish I could sit there. Ms. Maryann and Ms. Margaret wave from another table, and so do Mr. Jackson and Ms. Harper. Wish I could join any of them. Leo's mom is with someone who must be Leo's father because neither of them can take their eyes off Leo. I'd sit with the Corpuz family in a heartbeat.

A man walks to the microphone. "Friends, you're in for a treat tonight as you dine. Sunny Creek is now home to a future star in the music world, Leo Corpuz, a rising eighth grader who plays guitar like you've never heard it played before. And he's also the lead actor in our town's upcoming summer musical—*The Sound of Music*! Sit back, relax, and enjoy!"

Leo flashes his smile around the room and starts strumming. The music, magnified by the microphone, fills the restaurant with sweetness. I forget my embarrassment and even my irritation over The Intruder. I'm not the only one who's entranced. Leo thought people might be talking while he played, but nobody makes a sound. Candlelight flickers on listening faces. When the first song ends, the restaurant erupts into applause.

Waiters start serving food while Leo plays a few more wordless pieces. While people eat, a bit of conversation circulates around the room. I wish they'd shut up. Especially Baba and The Intruder, who are whispering and laughing like they're in some feel-good romantic comedy. Frustration roars up in my head. But Indy's imaginary voice comes in with a rebuttal: *When was the last time you heard Baba laugh like that? When was the last time he looked so happy?*

After dessert is served, Leo puts his guitar aside and stands up. "My last two songs have lyrics. They're written by other people because I'm not good with words."

"Yes, you are!" a voice calls out. Sounded like Katrina to me.

Leo grins and puts a hand to his heart.

"Wow, only thirteen and already gesturing like a stage pro," Shar says in a low voice.

"I'm nowhere near as good with lyrics as these two songwriters, that's for sure," Leo says. "One of them is the poet Emily Dickinson, who, unfortunately, couldn't be here tonight." The audience laughs. "It's called 'I'm Nobody! Who Are You?'"

My heart is in my throat. Our song will be his finale.

Leo delivers the Dickinson song as coolly as if we were on the porch of Orchard Manor. As applause erupts at the end of it, Indy puts two fingers in her mouth and out comes one of her piercingly loud whistles.

Leo stands again. "My last song is called 'Rain in the

Forest.' My friend Pandita Paul wrote the lyrics. There she is, over there." He points in my direction, and all the heads in the restaurant turn to me.

Suddenly, before I can talk them out of it, my legs push me up out of my chair. One hand even lifts in a little half wave. This new outfit, apparently, has given my body a mind of its own. As the audience applauds, I quickly sit down again. My family's eyes and mouths are as round as luchis. They're too surprised to say anything.

Leo waits until everyone settles down. And then he starts singing our song. His voice takes us into the forest's joyful rain dance. The scene *I* created. The last line lingers like a rainbow over the whole room, and then a thunder of cheers explodes in the restaurant. Even the waiters are clapping.

Baba leaps to his feet and drops a kiss on my head. "Pandu! That was amazing! I'm so proud of you."

"So beautiful, Pundit!" That's Indy.

"Finding your voice!" Shar is beaming.

"Wonderful, Pandu!" says The Intruder.

Joy fizzles away, and I feel like . . . a soda can left behind after one sip. This is my debut as a songwriter, the crowd is going wild, and now Ma—not some stranger named Shefali Som—should be here, smiling at me from across the table. *Ma* should be calling me by that special nickname, not this woman.

I can't stay here another second. "Thanks," I manage to say. "I should congratulate Leo." I get up and make my way through the crowd.

It takes a while because so many people stop me to say how much they loved our song. Just as his wife's had, Leo's father's welcoming smile puts me at ease right away. "So this is the girl I've been hearing so much about. Your poem was beautiful, my dear."

"Thank you, Mr. Corpuz. But it was all your son— you were SO GOOD!" I say, turning to Leo.

"Everyone seemed to think our song was the best one I played," he says. "Maybe you'll share another poem with me?"

I think of "Fog." I'd love to hear the music he might compose for that poem. "Sure," I say, beaming.

Katrina and Jemma walk over. "I'm so proud of you, Pandita," says Jemma, throwing her arms around me. "And you, too, of course, Leo!"

"You were fabulous," Katrina tells him. I can't help noticing she doesn't say anything to me. "And you must be Leo's father. So nice to meet you." Her manners are perfect with grown-ups.

"Same, same," says Leo's father. "Hello, Jemma. So kind of you and your mother to join us. Not all my wife's bosses have shown such support to Leo's music."

On the other side of the room, Nurse Corpuz and Mrs. Kim are talking to each other. I don't often think about Jemma's mom being Leo's mom's boss, but now I wonder if that makes a difference to him. Or to her. It doesn't seem to, but I sure hope their moms keep getting along. I don't need any more friendship stress in my life. And that's when I catch Jemma nudging Katrina.

Katrina shakes her head.

Jemma gives her an elbow dig.

Katrina sighs and takes a step toward me. "Er . . . want to join us for s'mores at Jemma's house?"

I hesitate. Does she really want me, or is it because Jemma's asking? Will they always be a package deal? But then, I remember how happy she was when Jemma got the lead. Plus, she *didn't* quit camp, even when her mother thought she should. Too bad she wasn't raised by a mother as sweet as mine. *Reading so many good stories has made you courageous and loving.* That's what *my* mother thought of me.

"I'd like that," I say. "I'll ask Baba to drop me off. See you there."

In the car, I whisper in Indy's ear. "Can we go shopping soon? I really like this dress. Maybe we should get me some more new clothes before school starts."

"Of course," Indy whispers back, trying and failing to hide her delight.

The Intruder is so much shorter than Ma that we only see her forehead over the headrest when she turns. "Where did you learn to write poetry, Pandu?"

This third time, the easy use of the nickname lands like a knockout punch. I swallow, hard. Reaching over, Shar grabs one of my hands and holds it tight. Thanks to her support, I muster a reply: "I like to write."

"Pandu's always been a reader, too," Baba says. "Started devouring books on her own when she was four."

Oh, thank goodness. We're at the Kims' house. Quickly, I say goodbye, pull my hand out of Shar's, and climb out of the car.

"Call when you need pickup," Indy says through the window. "AND HAVE FUN!"

I walk in the Kims' side gate like I used to so often, back when it was just Jemma and me. Now, what sounds like dozens of voices are chatting and laughing in the backyard. A bunch of kids from drama camp are sitting around the fire pit—Jenny, Joey, almost all of Team Hollywood, and a few people from other groups, too.

Leo gestures to an empty chair beside him at the fire, just as he does in the theater every day. As I take it, he hands me a long wire to use for s'mores. I skewer a marshmallow, spin it above the coals until it's brown, and sandwich it between graham crackers and chocolate. An owl hoots in the distance. Overhead, the summer stars are dazzling. Leo's arm brushes against mine every now and then. Someone starts singing "The Rose." Jemma, Katrina, and Leo sing, too, and after a while, so do I.

"Time for a joke-off," Jemma says once we're done with the song. She stands up. "You and me, von Trapp."

"Fine," Leo says, getting up to join her.

"What do you call a cow jumping over a barbed wire fence?" Jemma asks. And then: "An udder disaster."

Hisses and boos come from the listeners.

"Tough crowd," Jemma says. "Your turn, Captain."

Leo thinks for a minute. "What do you call a cow with two legs? Lean beef."

Loud groans.

Jemma doesn't hesitate. "What do you call a cow with no legs? Ground beef."

"Good one, Maria!" says Leo. "Where do cows get their medicine? At the *farm*-acy."

"Bada boom," says Jemma, giggling.

The rest of us are watching like spectators at a tennis match.

"What did the mother cow say to the baby cow?" Leo asks. He waits a beat. "It's pasture bedtime!"

Suddenly, Katrina jumps up, puts her hands on her hips, and rolls her eyes. "These jokes are so fourth grade. Eighth graders like us should watch a movie instead."

There's a silence. Nobody else seems to have caught the wordplay; she didn't stretch out the first syllable of the word *movie* enough. Her smile fades.

Her pun was actually more creative than a canned

joke, I think. I get up and stand next to her. "You're right, Katrina. A moooooovie would be great. Or maybe we should play truth or dairy."

Now everyone gets it. They laugh.

Katrina's dimples come back. "Or spin the carton," she says.

Jemma elbows both of us aside. "What do you call a cow that just had a baby?" she asks, looking around. And then: "De-*calf*-inated!"

That's when I snort; I can't help it. She looked so happy delivering the dumb punch line. My snort makes Jemma laugh, and Leo joins in. Out comes a high-pitched giggle from Katrina, which sounds so funny that everyone loses it.

# THIRTY-FIVE

SHAR HOSTS ANOTHER GOLDEN STATE Dwellings strategy meeting at our house. Indy's asked me to help her with snacks, so I'm handing out cookies. As usual, The Intruder is cuddling close to Baba on the couch. I'm getting good at averting my eyes this summer—from her *and* the property on sale across the street. And from Orchard Manor, too, when I pass it, even though I think about Mr. Marvin every time.

"The Johnson Family Trust has set the middle of August as their deadline to receive offers," Mr. Flemming is saying. "This means we have to keep going strong on fundraising. Where are we to date?"

Someone on the fundraising committee gives an update. They're about ninety percent of the way to offering market price.

"But the developers will probably come in way over that," Ms. Consuela says. "I think we need to—"

"You're counting on charity donations to buy this land?" It's HER. Interrupting. Again. "Ah, America. The land where people give money away so generously. What a mystery."

"Er, yes, and Sunny Creek citizens have been quite wonderful about it, along with some foundations as well," says Mr. Flemming. "But Consuela's right. Developers will put in higher offers no matter what we manage to raise. There's nothing we can do about that except hope that the seller miraculously chooses us. Any progress on contacting the owners?"

The college-aged woman named Julia answers. "We still can't find them," she says glumly.

"Keep working on it," says Mr. Flemming. "But even if that miracle happens and our offer is accepted, we'll still need to figure out how to get the Council to change the zoning at their September meeting. Zoning subcommittee?"

Shar stands. The fight-preservation subcommittee was dismantled after their success, and now she's in charge of this one. "The Council and mayor, of course, care what voters think, so we'll have to convince the citizens of Sunny Creek we need multi-family zoning in this neighborhood. But the town is split—some of them want it zoned for offices, and some to stay like it is: single-family residential with no rentals."

"The no-rental people are so shortsighted," Ms. Consuela says. "Housing costs will only go up in the future. Where will the next generation of Sunny Creek's teachers, police officers, and nurses live?"

Nurses? Like Leo's Mom? My heart speeds up a bit. The Corpuz family, living across the street from us in a townhouse? That. Would. Be. Amazing. It's been worrying me that Leo's father is pushing so hard for them to move. For the first time since the property was demolished, I feel like rooting for Shar's team. Especially if a win for them means Leo and his family stay in Sunny Creek.

"We need to brainstorm a publicity campaign," Mr. Flemming is saying. "Let's break up into committees."

As people start forming groups, The Intruder makes her way toward me, carrying a shopping bag. Maybe it's time to escape upstairs. Dropping the empty cookie plate on the coffee table, I practically run up to my room. But after a bit, there's a loud *rat-a-tat* on my door.

"Who is it?" As if I don't know.

"I have something for you."

Yep. It's *her*.

I get up and open the door. "Come in," I say, even though that's the last thing I want.

She enters swinging her bag and marches across the rug. Lofting the bag, she drops it on the bed and then plants herself—of all the places in the world—in my mother's rocking chair. I feel like screaming *GET UP!*

but the words stay inside me. I know in my gut that Ma would never have said them.

"What a superb room," The Intruder says, rocking back and forth as she glances around my last remaining sanctuary. "So old-fashioned and cozy. I especially love the desk. Open the bag, why don't you?"

I pull a shalwar chameez out of the shopping bag. It's a silky pink with white flowers embroidered all over it, and even without holding it up to my body I can tell it will fit. I spread it across the bed, lift the hem, and take a closer look. The stitching is perfect. She *is* a good sewer, and fast, too.

"Thanks. It's . . . pretty." But I put it back in the bag.

"You're so welcome. When you said you liked pink the other day, I remembered that an Aunty had given me this one. I've never worn it because the color doesn't suit me, so I altered it for you, Pandu."

It always sounds like a swear word when she says it. I can't help grimacing. Plopping down on my bed, I pick up the script of *The Sound of Music* from my nightstand. "I'll try it on later. I've got some memorizing to do. Thank you again."

I open the script.

But she's not that easy to dismiss.

Clearing her throat, she shifts in the rocking chair as if she's uncomfortable, or as if it doesn't really fit. "Maybe the two of us can go out for a meal sometime, Pandu—I mean, Pandita?"

So she *finally* got my body language about the nickname. Even so, I can't imagine eating a meal one-on-one with this person. "I'm pretty busy with drama camp. But thanks for asking."

"Yes, I can't wait to see your production. With that talented fellow, Leo, in the lead, it's going to be marvelous. He's a prodigy."

I turn the page, even though I haven't read a single word. "He doesn't like being called that. Says it makes it sound like he doesn't put in hours of time practicing, which he does."

"Of course. Anything worthwhile takes time to achieve."

There's a silence. I keep pretending to read the script, even though I know I'm bordering on rudeness.

She stands up, leaving the empty rocking chair swaying slightly. "Let's try and set a date for dinner together, just you and me."

Never. "Okay."

Once she's gone, I put the script back on my nightstand, head to my bookshelf, and find my copy of *The Silver Chair*. Narnia's always such a comfort when I need it. I've started reading newer books from the library, but I can still read old favorites too, right?

# THIRTY-SIX

THE WEEKEND BEFORE THE MUSICAL. Leo invites me to his family's apartment for lunch. Just me. No Jemma or Katrina.

As the day approaches, I'm nervous and zinging at the same time. Nervously zinging. Is that even possible?

"Keep breathing, Pundit," Indy says. "You'll be fine." She drops me off in front of the tall, blocky apartment building before heading to her department store, which is right down the street at the mall. We're planning to meet after lunch to do some shopping for me.

Leo comes out the front entrance, and I follow him into the small foyer. It smells like stale french fries, beer, and sweat in here, but I try not to scrunch up my nose in case Leo's watching. The elevator takes us to the fourteenth floor, where Leo's parents are waiting in an open doorway. All my anxiety is swept away by their warm hugs. Even the zinging settles down a bit. We take off our shoes to enter the apartment, which makes me feel even more at home.

The smells inside are amazing, and the feast spread

out on the small table makes me feel like royalty. Leo explains the food for me: lumpia, fresh vegetables wrapped in a springy, moist dough topped with peanut butter sauce, chicken adobo, which looks like what he sometimes brings to lunch at camp, a yummy sour soup with shrimp that Leo calls "sinigang," and a big bowl of steaming white rice. It's all delicious.

"The Asian staple," Mr. Corpuz says with a wink, and ladles another scoop of rice on my plate.

After we eat and talk about the upcoming musical, they share pictures and stories about their life in Manila. I laugh at chubby little Leo wearing nothing but diapers as he toddles around a garden.

"I've slimmed down," Leo says, helping himself to another lumpia.

His father reaches over to pinch his cheek. "There's still a bit of baby fat here and there."

"Tatay!" Leo protests, as Nurse Corpuz and I exchange a smile.

After lunch, when I ask to use the bathroom, Nurse Corpuz apologizes as she opens a door off the living room. "Sorry about the mess," she says. "One bathroom for the three of us and guests is not ideal."

"We need to move fast if we want to get that house, Alodia," Leo's father calls out from the table. It sounds like an old conversation between Leo's parents. They're still talking about where to live when I rejoin them.

"I found a perfect three-bedroom rental in San Jose," Mr. Corpuz tells me. "I know the high school there doesn't have a theater program like the one in Sunny Creek, but that house even has a garden. I say we get it, but these two want to stay in this tiny apartment until we find a better place in this town. Problem is, we'll never afford a decent place here. And I don't want Leo sleeping on a fold-out couch anymore."

"We might find a good rental in Sunny Creek, if Pandita's sister's organization gets their way," Leo says.

"Oh, if we could rent one of those new town-houses . . . ," Nurse Corpuz says, crossing herself. "If they get approved, and if we get on the wait-list, I'm willing to stay in this place until they're built."

"That's a lot of 'ifs,'" says Mr. Corpuz.

"I'm not giving up hope," she answers.

"Me, either," I say.

"I'm Team Hope, too," says Leo. "Can we stay if all those things happen, Tatay?"

"Yes, but they're not going to happen." Mr. Corpuz flips a hand at us. "Most of Silicon Valley doesn't want people like us living in their neighborhoods. They'll vote for mansions or offices."

"Silicon Valley used to be called the 'Valley of Heart's Delight,'" Leo tells his parents. "Tell them about the orchard, and about Lydia Johnson, Pandita."

No, thanks. Aunty Lydia's gone, and so are her house

and orchard. I glance at my watch. "Why don't you tell them? I have to meet my sister at the mall. Thank you so much for a delicious lunch."

I say goodbye to Leo's parents, and he walks me to the department store before heading home. So Captain von Trapp–ish.

I find Indy in the dressing room area of the young women's clothing section. She's wearing a name badge and gathering clothes that people have strewn on the floor and benches of the small stall.

"Have fun?" she asks me. "Wait, I can tell you did by that happy smile."

My smile gets even wider. I can't help it. It was such a good time.

"I want to hear all about it later, but for now, try these on," Indy says, pointing to a bunch of dresses, tops, and jeans that she's pushed to one side of the rack. "Baba gave me money this morning to shop for you. I think he was making up for how much he's saved buying T-shirts and overalls all these years. This means you can splurge a bit, plus my discount helps."

I try on the clothes she's picked for me, and when I like how something feels and looks, I come out and spin in front of the three-way mirror. Indy squints at me and weighs in between customers. I end up buying three dresses, five tops, a pair of jeans, and two skirts, none of which are as fancy as the ones Indy had picked out for me. They're going to take some getting used to, but most of the ones I pick feel as comfortable as my overalls. And it's a win-win, because they also have my sister's seal of approval.

"Wait in the shoe department," she tells me as she rings up my purchases. "I'll be done with my shift in an hour."

As I wander through the displays, my eyes land on a pair of sneakers with gold laces and a golden swoosh. When Indy joins me, we buy those and another pair of sandals like the ones she got me for my birthday.

Just before we leave the mall, she stops outside a salon.

"Let's get that hair trimmed for the musical," she says, eyeing my braids.

"It'll be hidden under my wimple."

"Not at the cast party," she says, ushering me to an empty chair.

"Just take off a bit, please," I tell the stylist. "I might not braid it as much, but I still like it long when it's loose."

The stylist opens and closes her scissors with a gleam in her eye. "You sure? I can give you a trendy cut like your sister's!"

"Absolutely not," I say firmly.

"Pandita's anything but trendy," Indy adds. "She's timeless."

"I can see that," the stylist says, and gets to work.

# THIRTY-SEVEN

EVERY CORNER OF OUR ONCE-PEACEFUL town is divided over the Johnson property. The pro-rental people are fighting with the office advocates. Both of those groups are battling the people who want our neighborhood to stay like it's been, with only a few larger houses on the Johnson lot. Signs pop up on neighbors' lawns and in storefronts, and arguments break out everywhere. A bunch of people at a bar even start a brawl that gets the police involved.

Ms. Maryann is in trouble, too. She put up posters advocating for Golden State Dwellings in the library, and her boss made her take them down.

"I guess he's right; we have to be neutral because we work for the town," she tells me. "But oh, I hope your sister and her friends win. Our Historical Society's split over the zoning issue, which is sad. Bev, Margaret, and I all want to see rental properties built, but Carol's joined the other side."

I think back to our first conversation about new-comers to Sunny Creek. Ms. Carol's alliance isn't surprising, but Ms. Margaret's is. Wasn't she talking about keeping out an "undesirable element" a few weeks ago? "What changed Ms. Margaret's mind?"

Ms. Maryann smiles. "Listening to you."

I remember the tears in Ms. Margaret's eyes when I was sharing about Aunty Lydia. Maybe that whole box-hunting expedition in Town Hall wasn't a total waste.

I check out a book called *Blubber* by Judy Blume, and Ms. Maryann gives me a quizzical look. "By now, you'd be rereading *Understood Betsy*, if I remember right. 'Out with the old, in with the new'?"

"I'm trying," I say. "It's not as easy as it sounds, though. Who said that, anyway?"

"Anonymous. But I like this quote better. Especially for you."

She hands me an index card that says *For Pandita* on it. I read the quote aloud: "'It has been said that, at its best, preservation engages the past in a conversation with the present over a mutual concern for the future.'"

"That was written by William Murtagh, first keeper of the National Register of Historic Places," she says. "That's what you can do for this town, Pandita."

"Me? How?"

"Just by being yourself. You know, even though you're wearing your hair loose these days, I've always loved those old-fashioned braids. They remind me that you, of all people, have an uncanny knack for weaving together past, present, and future."

I shrug, remembering my failure at the demolition hearing. "I don't think that's true, Ms. Maryann. But thanks for the vote of confidence, anyway."

I mull her words over as I walk home.

I'm reading new books, but when life gets stressful, I still prefer the familiar ones I've read at least ten times.

When it comes to style, I like my new clothes, but I haven't changed a thing in my room.

I'm all in now when it comes to seeing rental properties built across the street, especially if it means the Corpuz family might stay in town, but I desperately miss Ashar Jaiga.

I don't see Mr. Marvin anymore, but that makes me feel terrible, even though it *is* nice to have friends my age.

The Intruder's always around, and Baba seems happy. I still think about Ma and miss her all the time.

Ms. Maryann's wrong about this one. In the mixed-up life of Pandita Paul, past, present, and future feel more like a tangled knot than a tidy braid.

Tickets for our musical are sold out. By now, Leo and Jemma have their lines, singing, and even dancing down. They're going to be incredible. Katrina flounces around like a glamour queen, perfect as the Baroness. Joey and Jenny are ready. Jenny's littlest sister is adorable as the youngest von Trapp child, and their other two siblings are good, too.

It's just me, Pandita Paul, who isn't up to speed, and everybody at drama camp knows it. I've paid close attention to Ms. Harper's instructions on projection and enunciation. I've practiced my lines *and* Jemma's lines until everything is memorized. But none of that matters, because when my character starts talking to Sister Berthe and Sister Margaretta onstage, my voice still dwindles into a drone by the middle of my first scene: "I think we should be pleased with our efforts; out of twenty-eight postulants . . ." I'm not as bad as when we started, but nobody in the audience can hear much after the word "postulants."

"Let's try again, Pandita," says Ms. Harper. If she's exasperated with me, I don't hear it in her tone. "Musical cue, please, Mr. Jackson."

My second scene is a key one, where Pandita-Mother Abbess gives Jemma-Maria courage to return to the von Trapp family. I can sing "Climb Ev'ry Mountain" decently by now, hitting the high note almost every time, but when it comes to speaking it's almost as hard in this scene as in the other one. We have to keep repeating the lines again and again, even before Jemma enters. "Sister Sophia, take our new postulant to the robing room. Bless you, my daughter." The problem is that my voice gets low by the time I get to "postulant." I'm really starting to hate that word.

As the big night comes closer, I can tell that even Mr. Jackson is worried I won't be able to perform. He suggests placing a standing microphone at the foot of the stage for me. But Ms. Harper is adamant: "That will destroy the flow of the audience's imagination. Besides, Pandita will be able to project without a microphone. I know it in my bones."

"You're going to be fine, Pandita," adds Jemma, but it sounds like she's delivering a line from the script.

I really, really want to quit.

The day before our dress rehearsal, I suggest it, but Katrina puts her fists on her hips and comes closer until she's four inches away from me. "That's the most selfish, cowardly thing I've heard in a long time, Pandita Paul. If you left now, all of us would have to scramble. Besides, if anything happens to Jemma before opening night, *you're* the only one who knows her part."

I look at Leo for support, but he shrugs. "She's speaking truth, Pandita."

Jemma is nodding, too.

Ugh. They're right. Besides, even with my failures and stage fright, I'm enjoying drama camp. For the first time in what feels like forever, I have friends my age.

And they need me.

# THIRTY-EIGHT

ANOTHER LETTER FROM BAKKHALI SHOWS up in the mailbox. Our grandparents are as faithful in writing their monthly letters as . . . wait for it . . . a nun in keeping her vows.

After reading it, I sit with a blank lavender notecard and my favorite pen, but composing a reply is harder than it used to be. Didu and Dadu don't want to hear how The Intruder and Baba spend almost every day together. And how in the evenings, too, she's in our home, sharing recipes from her mother in Calcutta with Indy. Why would Ma's parents want to hear about that?

Instead, I fill up the notecard with news about the musical and end with this:

*I know Ma used to sing and dance in front of a crowd on festival days in Bakkhali. Did she ever get stage fright when she performed? If I didn't have to SPEAK, I'd be fine. My friends Leo and Jemma are so good in their lead roles. I want the audience to remember THEIR performances, not leave thinking about a girl who froze up and couldn't say a word. I wish you were here to see the show and give me moral support. Forever Yours, Pandu.*

When I bring the letter from our grandparents down to share, our entire kitchen smells and looks like it's in the city of Calcutta, not in Sunny Creek, California. Shar's watching Indy make pakoras. They're both wearing shalwar chameez outfits that The Intruder made, which fit perfectly. And the seamstress herself is once again on my favorite stool. Baba is nowhere in sight.

"Come, Pandita," she says, patting the empty stool where Baba usually sits. "Your sister is making my mother's recipe along with a batch of her usual pakora. We're about to taste them both and make our judgments."

I don't sit down. "Oh. Here's the latest letter from Bakkhali," I announce, as Indy puts two plates of pakora on the kitchen table.

"Do you have relatives there?" The Intruder asks. "It's quite a remote village. One of our housemaids had to take a train for eight hours to reach Calcutta from Bakkhali."

The three of us don't answer for a bit. Then, Shar says: "Our mother was born and raised in that village."

Another silence.

Indy breaks it this time by picking up a pakora from each of the plates and taking a bite of each one. "Oh, yum. They're equally amazing."

The Intruder tastes both kinds of pakora, too. "Ah, but in my mother's recipe, the cumin comes through a bit more."

Indy takes another bite of the first one, then the other, frowning as she chews. "You're right. I'm not sure if I like that better, though." She changes the subject. "So, Pundit, are you ready for the big night? It's only two days away!"

I gulp. Two nights is all I have left for a miracle to happen.

"Oh, how I love *The Sound of Music*!" The Intruder says, turning to me. "I can't wait to see your rendition. I've seen the film so many times."

Wait, what? She's watched *The Sound of Music* on repeat?

She reaches for another of Indy's pakoras. "I love old books and movies, don't you? It made me so happy to see you reading *The Secret Garden* the other day. I still reread it every spring. It belongs in the springtime just as *Little Women* belongs in the winter."

*And* she knows two of my favorite books? And rereads them again every year? *Seasonally*, like I do?

"You and Pundit definitely have that in common," Indy says, to cover my silence. "She's always reading old books."

"Really? Tell me, what else do you read, Pandita? The Chronicles of Narnia? The Betsy-Tacy books?"

Uncanny. It's like she's been stalking my library account. Or my bookshelves. Maybe she has.

"Nowadays I read new books," I say. "Old books, old clothes, old places, old people—I'm trying my best to leave them behind."

The Intruder shrugs. "I'll never stop reading *The Secret Garden*."

Shar glances at Indy with an expression I can't interpret but I know is about me. Sometimes I can't stand how much they care.

"So, how *was* rehearsal?" Shar asks.

"Terrible."

"What's going on?" Indy asks.

"The same thing that happened at that stupid Council meeting," I say. "My voice keeps dying."

"Hasn't Ms. Harper given you extra coaching?" Shar asks.

"Yes, but I'm useless at speaking. I can write; I should have stuck to that!"

The Intruder stands to face me. She's so short she has to tilt her chin up to look me in the eye. "It's important for women to speak boldly, especially in front of men. You, my dear, bear the name of the great Pandita Ramabai, who delivered a brilliant speech in front of two thousand male delegates at the National Social Congress in Bombay in 1889—the first woman ever to speak there."

I knew my namesake had fought for justice for widows and orphans, but I've never heard about this event. "She did?"

"She waited until the entire auditorium quieted down, and then announced: 'It is not strange, my countrymen, that my voice is small, for you have never given a woman the chance to make her voice strong!' After that, she had those men in the palm of her hand. They laughed and cried, and when she was finished, they rose to their feet to give her a rousing ovation."

Wow. Must have been some speech. I flash back to standing wordlessly in front of Mr. Reed. The Intruder has a point about being able to speak in front of powerful men.

I pop a pakora in my mouth. After I chew and swallow, I take a swig of water and sample a pakora from the other plate. "These are both yummy," I say, sounding like . . . wait for it . . . like a judge announcing a verdict that's surprising even to her.

# THIRTY-NINE

LEO AND I SHOW UP early to dress rehearsal the next evening, so we're in the cafeteria alone for once. Some kids' parents are prepping a pizza party. It's nice, having a few minutes just the two of us before Jemma and Katrina arrive.

"I'm going to bomb, Leo. I just know it."

"Remember what Ms. Harper said about fake-smiling to fool your brain into thinking you aren't scared."

A parent plops a pizza carton on our table, and Leo opens it.

I help myself to a slice. "Did you know there's actually a word that means 'fear of public speaking'? I looked it up. 'Glossophobia.' I'm glossophobic, Leo."

He drops his piece of pizza on his plate, lifts both hands, and lets air out through gritted teeth.

"What's wrong?"

"I didn't want to put pressure on you. But I think I have to, now. You can't go around telling the rest of us how nervous you are, Pandita. Other performers pick up on the anxiety."

"Oh. I don't want that."

"What you need is someone outside drama camp *and* your family to boost your confidence. Someone you can trust to be impartial. Like . . . Mr. Marvin, for example? Maybe you should stop by and deliver your lines to him. *I've* been rehearsing with him, and he's been very encouraging. I even invited him to our show."

Another harried-looking parent sets down a bottle of soda and some plastic cups on our table. I fill two cups and hand one to Leo. "I'm done visiting Orchard Manor."

"Why?"

"We got in a . . . well, a spat, I guess."

"I'm sure he's feeling bad about that. He keeps asking about you. And he wants *me* to find old children's books for him now. I have no idea what he'd like."

I was going to introduce my ex–old–best friend to *The Secret Garden* next, but I don't tell Leo that. Instead, I sip my soda and fend off a wave of sadness.

Jemma and Katrina come in.

"You're wrong, Katrina Reed!" Jemma is saying as they join our table.

"You just don't get it, do you?" Katrina shoots back.

Jemma and Katrina arguing? This is new.

"Nice shoes, you two," I say, sliding over to make

room for Katrina. They're wearing tennis shoes with gold decor—the same as mine. They ran over to Kleg-man's after watching me waltz in my new pair.

"Thanks," says Jemma, sitting down next to Leo and helping herself to a piece of pizza.

"What were you two talking about?" I ask.

"Town politics, believe it or not," Jemma answers.

"She's upset that my father's trying to protect our nice, safe town!" Katrina's voice is louder than usual. For the first time since we've become friends, it reminds me of her mother's.

Jemma pours some soda. "At first Umma was against building new rental properties, too, but now that she's been hunting for a nicer apartment in town for Leo's family, she's changed her mind."

Katrina looks a little embarrassed. "I don't think my parents thought of people like the Corpuz family mov-ing into those townhouses. They're just nervous that the town might change."

"Maybe Sunny Creek needs to change," I say.

"Change isn't always for the better," says Katrina.

I have a déjà vu moment as I hear myself echoed in her words—they're exactly what I said to Shar before the demolition.

"If it happens, it happens," Leo says. "If it doesn't, my parents will figure something out. For now, we're still in Sunny Creek. At least for the rest of the summer."

The three of us stop eating.

"What do you mean, the rest of the summer?" I ask.

Leo clears his throat. "Nanay got a job offer at a senior center out in Stockton."

"WHAT?" Katrina's iced tea sloshes onto the table.

I can't say anything. I can't even look at Leo.

"Is she going to take it?" Katrina asks, wiping up the spill with a napkin.

"She hasn't yet. It's less pay, but we could afford a nice house and we have relatives there. Tatay's sent his résumé out to a couple of schools and we're waiting for them to reply. You can't tell your mom yet, Jemma. Promise?"

She nods.

I still can't speak.

"What do you think, Pandita?" he asks. "Would you come and visit? We could write, too. I know how much you like letters."

I look up and into his eyes of copper. "There's still a chance the property could be zoned for rentals. And if that happens, Shar says they'll be taking applications right away. If your family gets on the list for one of those townhouses, would your parents stay in Sunny Creek?"

"I'm not sure," Leo says, but then he gives me a sliver of hope. "Maybe."

Then that's what has to happen.

# FORTY

THE DRESS REHEARSAL IS A disaster. The parent in charge of makeup gets in a fender bender on the way to the school and doesn't show up. Of course, she has all our makeup in her car. The costumes for the nuns and Nazis are in her car, too, so we have to rehearse in tie-dyed T-shirts. Katrina bungles her lines, Leo knocks over one of Jenny's little sisters while dancing, and Jemma rips her governess dress squirming into it backstage.

And me? I have such a bad case of stage fright that I can barely breathe, let alone talk. At least Jemma's as healthy as a horse . . . no, wait for it . . . oh, forget it, I'm too nervous to think of a better simile.

Right before I leave, Ms. Harper pulls me aside for one last pep talk. "Remember before your audition, when I asked you to engage your well-oiled imagination? Well, I'm not sure you took my advice then, but that's exactly what you need to do now. Break it down like this: First, imagine someone else, someone you admire, speaking boldly in front of an audience, and try to imitate that person's presence. Second, and we've talked about this nonstop for days, imagine that you ARE the character you're playing. Before the curtain opens, *become* Mother Abbess. You want the best for Maria, right?"

I nod. I do that a lot around Ms. Harper.

"And here's the third and last task for your excellent imagination, Pandita. I've saved it for now, so listen closely. Stage fright mostly comes from fear of an unknown audience's reaction, so I want you to picture one person who loves you thoroughly and unconditionally watching your performance. If you do that, I think you'll move from stage fright to being in the moment. And that's why they call it 'stage PRESENCE.'"

During the last waking hours before our show, I do exactly as Ms. Harper says. First, I picture Pandita Ramabai in front of a crowd of men, speaking boldly on behalf of widows and orphans. I think of Aunty Lydia, fighting for the Ichiuji family while they were interned. And when I get into my wimple and someone on the makeup team artfully adds wrinkles to my face, I do feel like Mother Abbess. No, I *am* Mother Abbess, and Jemma isn't Jemma; she's Maria, a young postulant I'm trying to help.

Last of all, right before the curtain opens, I take a big breath and picture my beautiful mother in the front row, watching with pride and delight.

❀ ❀ ❀

Turns out our drama teacher was right.

Magic *does* happen in a theater.

During my first scene, I manage to project my spoken voice, if not to the back row, at least to the middle of the auditorium.

"I did okay!" I tell Leo backstage, and he gives me a hug for the first time ever. It's a little awkward with my nun's habit crushed between us, but I'm too excited to notice.

At intermission I peek through the curtain. Leo's parents and Mrs. Kim are here, and so are my sisters, Baba, and his perpetual date. Ms. Maryann and the other Historical Society members are scattered throughout the audience. There's no sign of Mr. Marvin. Why wouldn't he make an effort to come for Leo's sake, after all the hymns and scones he's enjoyed thanks to the Corpuz family?

I could have talked him into it, if we were still friends.

He would have loved the show.

He would have loved seeing Leo in the show.

And he might even have enjoyed seeing me in it, too.

I let the gap in the curtain close and concentrate on getting ready for my second scene. Jemma and I make it through our lines, even though I'm not as loud as I was during my first scene. But when I sing "Climb Ev'ry Mountain," my voice soars into the audience, sweet and high, past the front row, where Ma beams in my imagination, all the way up to the balcony, where my family is sitting. I hold the high note perfectly because I *am* Mother Abbess, and I *do* want Maria to find her dream.

When I'm done, the applause goes on and on.

Smiling from one side of my wimple to the other, I float off the stage.

Backstage, I pump my fist in the air. Jemma and Katrina race over to smother me in hugs. "You did great!" they whisper, beaming.

The musical rolls to the end, and despite some mistakes here and there, we're clearly a hit. The applause is deafening as the cast and crew emerge onstage after the final curtain. When I step out to take my own personal bow, I hear Indy's piercing whistle, and The Intruder's booming voice calls out, "HOORAY FOR PANDITA!"

The cast party at Jemma's house lasts until two in the morning.

And with that, drama camp, which I'd been dreading so fervently, is behind me.

# FORTY-ONE

WITH THE MUSICAL OVER, JEMMA at her church sleepaway camp, and Katrina on her family's annual Hawaii vacation, I have time to join the fight for rental properties. I clutch a picket sign next to Shar outside the grocery store and the post office. I help post flyers around town and show up at every one of Golden State Dwellings' meetings.

Leo joins us every now and then, too. One evening, the two of us are setting up folding chairs around the living and dining rooms. Mr. Flemming has called an emergency gathering. As people start to come in, we find two chairs in the back by the kitchen. Leo takes his guitar out and starts strumming quietly. He's working nonstop on tunes for my winter tree and fog poems because during camp, he didn't have much time to compose. I get that; I haven't come up with any new poems this summer, and my fingers are itching to write. Once this battle over the property across the street is over, I'll make the time again.

As the meeting gets underway, Baba comes home and enters quietly through the swinging door. He has dark shadows under his eyes, his hair is rumpled, and he definitely hasn't shaved in a couple of days. The Intruder isn't with him. In fact, she hasn't been around the last three nights. Is she okay? Suddenly, I wonder if she's decided to *stop* intruding.

"I'll be in my study," Baba whispers when he comes to drop a kiss on my head. I'll have to find out later why his face looks so . . . demolished.

"Offers are due by the end of this month," Mr. Flemming reminds the somber crowd jammed into our living and dining rooms. "What's our total amount in the bank?"

A few people cheer when they hear the fundraising subcommittee's answer, including Leo and me. It's exactly what the property is listed for.

Mr. Flemming raises his hand to stop our celebration. "I hate to say this, but the owners probably won't choose our offer, even at market price, because we're never going to outbid the developers. Their offers have gone sky-high over the past week."

The room quiets down; faces look blank.

"All this work for nothing," Shar says. "It's going to be so hard watching them build only eight huge houses on that big piece of land."

It was terrible watching them demolish what used

to be there. But Shar's right—seeing big houses getting built across the street *is* going to be hard, because it means the Corpuz family will leave Sunny Creek. I have no idea if Aunty Lydia's descendants are making these decisions, but I fight a surge of anger at them. Not only did they demolish her orchard and house, they're letting her values be violated, too. I remember how she housed the Sanchez and Martinez families. I'm sure that if she were selling the land, she'd choose Golden State Dwellings as the buyer.

The room is unusually quiet. This very vocal group of people has run out of words. All we can hear now is Leo's gentle strumming.

I look around at the sad faces. "Sing something for us, Leo?" I ask.

As usual, he doesn't hesitate. He starts playing a bit more loudly, and I recognize the song right away; he'd finished it before the musical got underway. It's that Dickinson poem—"'Hope' is the thing with feathers."

*Hope is the thing with feathers*
*That perches in the soul,*
*And sings the tune without the words,*
*And never stops at all . . .*

The music and words float around the room. When the song ends, the silence doesn't feel as heavy. After a bit, Mr. Flemming stands. He's smiling now. "Well, you heard the song, people. We don't stop hoping, no matter what. Back to our tasks."

As the crowd divides into committees, I beam at Leo. "Good choice."

"Dickinson's okay, but it's easier to set Pandita Paul poems to my kind of music."

Now my heart feels like it's floating, too.

Once everyone's gone, I knock on Baba's study door.

"Come in," I hear him answer.

He's sitting in the dark, listening to Bengali music on his cassette recorder.

"What's wrong, Baba?" I ask, switching on the light and walking over to put a hand on his shoulder.

"Nothing, Pandu."

I wait, keeping my hand where it is. *Your quiet, listening spirit helps me share things I keep deep inside.*

Baba sighs. "Well, if you want to know the truth, Shef and I . . . ended our friendship. I mean . . . well, she asked if I intended to marry her, given all the time we were spending together, and I told her no."

I'd been wanting this to happen all along, but now that it has, I feel sad for Baba. He looks so crushed; his face is as empty as the Johnson property across the street. "Oh, Baba. I'm sorry."

He pats my hand. "Don't worry, Pandu. I'll be fine, I promise. I'm just a little down for now. Tell your sisters for me, will you? But please don't mention the proposal; they'd make a fuss about that."

When I tell my sisters about the breakup later that night, they look almost as shocked as when I told them that she kissed him.

"What happened?" Indy asks.

"They were crazy about each other," Shar says.

I hesitate, and my voice gets low. "Maybe it's my fault. I wasn't as welcoming to her as you were."

Twin talk. And then: "No, Pundit, I struggled, too," Shar says.

"You both did the best you could," Indy says firmly. "I think this is about his own guilt. And his grief. It has nothing to do with either of you."

But I'm not convinced. Baba might have ended things with her for his own reasons, but I didn't help.

I didn't try on the shalwar chameez she made for me.

I didn't follow up on her dinner invitation for just the two of us. And now I probably never will.

Strange how without her loud laugh and strong opinions, the house feels a little too quiet.

# FORTY-TWO

ONE HOT AUGUST DAY, A postcard instead of an aerogramme shows up in our mailbox. On the front is a photo of a man with big eyes and a long white beard. The caption says: Rabindranath Tagore, Bard of Bengal, Nobel Laureate. I turn it over to read what's on the back.

*Beloved Pandu. Thank you for telling us about your performance in the musical. Kudos to a poet courageous enough to take risks in another realm of art! How we wish we could have been there to witness your theatrical triumph! Our hearts are soaring with pride.*

Most of the rest of the words on the postcard are in Bangla, set up line by line like a poem. But there's one more line in English:

*In honour of what would have been your mother's 38th birthday, please enjoy this poem by another Bengali poet who was a risk-taker.*

Suddenly, I can't breathe.

Ma's birthday.

I used to write a longer letter to her on that day, sitting on Aunty Lydia's porch swing at Ashar Jaiga.

I've been so busy with the musical and Leo and Golden State Dwellings—and our special place is gone. But that doesn't excuse this.

Oh, Ma. Oh, my darling Ma.

I *am* starting to forget.

Clutching the postcard, I take it into the kitchen where Baba is sitting on his stool staring into space. A cold, full cup of coffee is in front of him.

"Will you translate this poem for me, Baba? It's in Bangla."

"Sure." He takes the card and looks at the photo of the bearded poet. "Tagore. Must be from your grandparents."

Flipping it over, he reads it, and his face gets even sadder than it already was, if that's possible. "I can't believe it, but I forgot her birthday this year."

"Me, too, Baba." I give him a hug. "Do you know the poem?"

"It's a famous one that Tagore set to music," he says. "It's called 'Purano Shey Diner Kotha,' which roughly means . . . 'Talk of Old Days.' Your mother used to sing this all the time. I think I even have a recording of her singing it somewhere."

"I want to know the meaning of the lines," I say. "I *need* to know them."

"Give me some paper and a pen and I'll give it a try. I'll need your help, though. It's poetry; you're the expert at that, not me."

Line by line, Baba and I struggle through the stanzas. I adjust the sound of a phrase and as he explains the meaning of a Bangla word, I find a better one in English. Once we're both satisfied, I read our translation out loud.

*All those old days.*
*All those old times.*
*Who forgets them, O my heart?*
*Eyes meeting,*
*Laughing, talking,*
*Who can forget that?*
*In morning's first light,*
*We picked our flowers.*
*We swung up so high.*
*I played my flute,*
*You sang your tunes,*
*In the shady trees.*

And then the chorus, again:

*All those old days.*
*All those old times.*

*Who forgets them, O my heart?*
*Eyes meeting,*
*Laughing, talking,*
*Who can forget that?*

The last verse is the saddest.

*When a parting came,*
*You went your way*
*And I went mine.*
*When we come together, O my love,*
*Rest inside my heart.*

"Good work, Pandu," Baba says, standing up to drop his signature kiss on my head. "I think our translation does Tagore justice. Or at least doesn't totally wreck the beauty of his poem."

I take stock of his tired, empty face as he reaches for my grandparents' postcard and reads it again. I so, so want to help Baba. But how? With a jolt, I remember what Indy said to me when she agreed to talk about Ma: "He has to let go one day, Pundit. We all do, even though it's so, so hard." I didn't want to admit it then, but she was right.

And then an idea comes.

"Baba, there's a box in the garage that you marked 'private' with some of Ma's things in it. May I . . . open it?"

I'm not sure he's listening. "Okay," he answers, then puts the card on the table and trudges out of the kitchen.

# FORTY-THREE

WHAT A SUMMER OF BOXES this is turning out to be. *And* letters. Making my way through the mess in the garage again, I pull out the box marked ASHA. KEEPERS. PRIVATE. It's heavy. Grateful my sisters aren't around to ask questions, I haul it up to my room.

After I slit the tape and fold back the flaps, I pull out a few books, both in Bangla and English, and five carousels of slides. Baba doesn't take photos with his fancy slide camera these days. In fact, he doesn't take photos at all; Indy does it now with her Instamatic and gets them developed at the drugstore. I catch sight of something small at the bottom of the box. It's a single cassette tape. It's labeled TAGORE SONGS. ASHA PAUL.

I race to Baba's study and bring back the slide projector and cassette player. Plugging the projector in, I aim the square of light at my closet door.

Then I drop in the first carousel.

Oh, wow.

Here she is, wearing a saree and sweeping the front

porch. The projector magnifies the photo so that it's much larger than the ones in the frames and albums downstairs. You can see details in these slides, like the way her eyes smiled along with her mouth, and how loose wisps of hair fell out of her bun.

I keep clicking through the carousel, eyes transfixed on my closet door. My throat is tight; after a while, I reach for a tissue to dab away the tears. Baby versions of Indy and Shar are curled on Ma's lap. All three are asleep, but it looks like the twins are tied into the safety of her saree somehow. As the carousel turns in a circle, I see the three of them again and again, the twins getting older, playing ring-around-the-rosy in the yard, planting trees in the garden, their first day of nursery school.

When the picture of Ma sweeping shows up again, I take that carousel out and put in the next one. This, too, is full of memories of Ma, Baba, and my sisters. It isn't until the third carousel that I show up. Somewhere in the middle of it, after Ma's stomach swells over time, there's a shot of the twins gazing adoringly at swaddled, tiny me. Soon, Ma is carrying a toddler version of me, fast asleep and clad in overalls, up the stairs.

On and on our family changes, traveling through the first nine years of my life. Until . . . we go to India. The last carousel has a few slides of the five of us in Calcutta with Baba's parents, and then in Bakkhali, with Didu and Dadu.

But there the photos stop.

I turn off the projector.

Time for the cassette tape. Popping it into the player and keeping the volume low, I lean close to the speakers. Then I press play. Even though I know what's coming, my heart leaps at the sound of her voice.

Oh, her voice!

Entrancing and soft.

Familiar and sweet.

Even with her lilting accent, the tone of it *does* sound like mine.

I miss it so much. I miss her so much.

I keep listening, hoping to hear the song my grandparents sent. Will it be here? And then it comes. It's the last song on the tape. "Purano Shey Diner Kotha," sings Ma's melodious voice, and memory floods my brain, my heart, my entire body—Ma, in the rocking chair in my room, singing this very song.

I play it again and again, matching our English translation to my mother's Bangla until it almost feels like I understand the Bangla. Strangely, slowly, Ma's voice and the words start to bring a deep sense of comfort.

*All those old days.*
*All those old times.*
*Who forgets them, O my heart?*
*Eyes meeting,*

*Laughing, talking,*
*Who can forget that?*
*When a parting came,*
*You went your way*
*And I had to go mine.*
*When we come together, O my love,*
*Rest inside my heart.*

I think of what Mr. Marvin said about mothers remembering us: *The mind might forget but the heart doesn't.* Heart to heart, Ma and I are woven together.

# FORTY-FOUR

THE NEXT DAY. I REWRITE the English translation of Tagore's song on a piece of lavender-scented stationery and add a note to my grandparents at the bottom:

*Dear Didu and Dadu. Thank you for the Tagore poem. Here is our translation. I hope you like it. I'll send one of my own poems in my next letter. Love, Pandu.*

After sealing the letter into an envelope and adding stamps, I pick up the index card that Ms. Maryann gave me. *It has been said that, at its best, preservation engages the past in a conversation with the present over a mutual concern for the future.*

That's exactly what I'm about to try with my family. But first I dial Leo's number and ask him to come over with his guitar.

"Is another Pandita poem coming my way?" he asks.

"Sort of. You'll see."

As soon as Leo arrives, I hand him the translation and

play the recording of Ma singing the song in Bangla on Baba's cassette player.

"Your mother had a beautiful voice, Pandita," Leo says, his eyes looking deep into mine.

I don't avert them. Let him see what he sees. It's messy, but it's real. "I miss it so much. I miss her every moment. Leo, will you help me tweak these English words to fit the tune? I want to sing it for my family."

As always, he's eager to help. I listen and wait as he figures out the music and lyrics. Then we sing through the song together several times. After a while, it sounds almost as good in English as it did when Ma sang it in Bangla. Almost, but not quite.

"Thank you, Leo, thank you!"

"You can pay me back in poems," he says with a smile. But then that smile fades. And *he* averts *his* eyes. He hesitates. Swallows. Continues.

"Yesterday, Tatay also got a job offer in Stockton. He wants us to move the first week of September so I can start eighth grade out there. Nanay's going to submit her resignation to Orchard Manor before the end of the month."

My stomach plummets. "Oh, no, Leo. Can't they wait and see what happens with the property? Shar and her team are working so hard."

He shakes his head sadly. "Sometimes the thing with feathers stops singing."

Not me, I think. I'm sticking to hope.

After Leo leaves, I start organizing the best slides into one carousel.

❧ ❧ ❧

Sunday evening is the only summer day left on the calendar that's free for my sisters and Baba. "The four of us are having dinner together," I tell them. They seem surprised, but nobody puts up a fuss.

"I'll cook something special," Indy says.

That leaves only one thing to do—officially revoke the pact my sisters and I made three years ago. My chance to be alone with Indy and Shar comes Saturday morning, when they're both in the kitchen before heading out for work.

I take my stool and a big breath at the same time. "Listen, you two, I think it's time to revoke our pact. Formally, I mean."

My sisters exchange one of their "What's going on with Pundit now?" looks.

"Is this about the breakup?" Indy asks.

"Kind of." Then I decide to turn the tables and ask a question of my own. "What do you think about revoking it, Shar?"

"Well . . . Baba *has* been walking around here like a zombie," says Shar. "And . . . well, I never thought I'd say this, but I miss Dr. Som!"

"So do I!" says Indy.

"Yeah . . . me, too," I admit. "Indy, you were the one who said talking about it might ease Baba's grief. I think Ma would have wanted us to help him move forward. Shouldn't we at least try?"

I put my hand on the kitchen table, palm down.

Slowly, Indy places hers on mine, and Shar's lands on top of the pile.

On Sunday afternoon, I open the other box in the garage and take Ma's green-and-white shalwar chameez upstairs to my room. When I put it on, it's a little big, but not by much. Carrying the projector and tape player downstairs, I arrange them in the living room before entering the kitchen.

My sisters gasp when they take stock of how I'm dressed. Baba's eyes widen.

"That's Ma's, right?" Indy asks.

I nod. "I found it in the garage. I think her shalwars will be too long for you two, but you might want to have a look at her sarees."

"This one fits you almost perfectly," Shar says.

"Baba? What do you think?"

"It's lovely, Pandu."

But I notice that after that first look, he keeps his eyes away.

Indy serves up lentils, rice, and shrimp curry. It *is* special. And delicious. After the dishes are done, I clear my throat.

"Will you guys join me in the living room? I have a surprise."

The projector is set up and aimed at the wall next to the television. I've taken down the framed batik that usually hangs there. The tape of Ma singing is cued up in the cassette player.

"You three sit on the sofa," I tell my family as they follow me out of the kitchen.

"A Baba sandwich," Indy says, plopping down on one side of him while Shar does the same on the other.

Baba slings an arm around each of them. "Ah! This is the life."

But then he sees the projector on the coffee table. His eyes travel to the cassette player. Suddenly, his face looks like the blank wall in front of us. "Ay, Bhagavan," he mutters.

I settle on the floor at his feet. Taking one of Ms. Harper's big pre-performance inhales, I start the show and the recording of Ma singing simultaneously.

At the first sound of Ma's voice, in perfect twin chore-ography, my sisters each put a hand on my shoulder. Baba's hands are clutched on his lap as he leans forward, too. I can see his profile now, and his jaw is clenched, but I don't press pause or stop.

Halfway through the carousel of photos, Ma's song ends. I turn off the cassette recorder and stand up. Then, just as Leo and I practiced, I click through slides while I sing the English version of the song that we tweaked to fit Rabindranath Tagore's music.

My family doesn't move or react, but I can tell they're taking in the words.

My song ends.

The carousel stops whirling.

The last slide is of the five of us in Bakkhali, smiling into the camera with no thought of the catastrophe that's about to crash into our family.

I leave it on the wall.

Suddenly, with a groan that sounds more like an animal than a human, Baba hides his face in his hands.

I can see his chest heaving.

Ay, Bhagavan.

I've broken my dear father's heart. Indy's grip tightens on my shoulder. I reach for the projector to make the photo disappear, but before I can turn it off, Baba lifts his head.

"Leave it," he says.

And then, face twisted and wet, body shuddering, breath coming in ragged gasps, he keeps his eyes on the photo and weeps.

It's terrible to watch.

Part of me wants to run away.

Escape into my room and put a pillow over my head. Get as far away from his grief as I can.

But something—someone?—keeps me in place. And Indy and Shar aren't moving, either. How long we sit there I don't know. Time, I think, might have stopped.

Bit by bit, Baba stops crying. As he exhales a few last, long, shivering sighs, Indy jumps up and brings back a tissue box. All four of us reach for a tissue at the same time. We laugh, but it's shaky. The box gets passed around. We blow our noses and mop up our faces.

Once his breath is back to normal, Baba clears his throat. "Pandu, that was . . . hard, but wonderful. So many happy memories. What a life the five of us had together, didn't we?"

"A wonderful one," says Shar.

"Magnificent," says Indy.

"So beautiful that it's hard to give up," I say.

Baba smiles at me. "But we have to, right? Pundit, I'm glad your grandparents sent that poem. You know, maybe it's time to take a trip back to Bakkhali."

I nod. "Definitely. Next summer would be good—before these two leave for college. And . . . I think Didu and Dadu would like to meet Dr. Som, too."

His eyebrows go up. "I don't think so, Pandu. We haven't spoken in a while."

I pat his hand. "Just tell her you changed your mind

and that you accept her proposal, Baba. India would be a good place to get married, don't you think?"

My sisters almost fall off the sofa as they swivel to confront him.

"*She* proposed to *you*? When? How? Tell us everything!" Indy, of course.

"You didn't accept? Oh, come *on*, Baba! What were you thinking?!" Shar opens her palms and her eyebrows go up—a signature move.

He looks at them, and then at me. "You *all* want me to say yes? Even you, Pandu?"

I think of the short, bubbly woman with the loud voice. She loves *The Secret Garden* as much as I do, and *Little Women*, the Betsy-Tacy books, the Narnia series. Even when I was pushing her away, she took the time to alter that shalwar chameez for me. But the best part is how happy Baba is around her.

"*Especially* me," I say.

# FORTY-FIVE

A FEW DAYS LATER, WHEN Jemma gets back from camp, I tell her the news about Baba's engagement.

"She's nothing like your mother," Jemma says. "But I'm happy if you are."

"I know. But that's okay."

We talk about how we're going to spend the rest of the summer, going out on Katrina's boat when she gets back, and she tells me everyone wants me to join the theater club when school starts. Neither of us want to bring up the sad fact that the Corpuz family is moving. I'm still in denial, even though offers on the Johnson property are due in just a few days and the developers continue to outbid one another. The odds that the unknown buyer will choose a much lower offer from Golden State Dwellings are shrinking by the day. And even if that happens, building rentals across the street depends on the Council changing the zoning for our neighborhood.

Things look bleak.

But I'm not giving up.

I'm not letting myself imagine Sunny Creek without Leo.

One afternoon, the two of us are sitting in the park by the fountain. He's strumming his guitar, as usual, and I'm trying to tweak my Thief of Time poem. It's hard to fine-tune the words without reading them aloud to the right pair of ears.

"Mr. Marvin isn't doing too well," Leo says, making me wonder if he's starting to read my mind. I sure hope not.

"Maybe he found out your mother's thinking of quitting," I say.

"I think it's something else. He doesn't talk much at all these days. Not even to her."

I could always get Mr. Marvin to talk. Suddenly, the words from the Tagore poem swing through my mind:

*All those old days.*
*All those old times.*
*Who forgets them, O my heart?*
*Eyes meeting,*
*Laughing, talking,*
*Who can forget that?*

I miss him. I miss reading my poetry to him. Maybe I'll try visiting him one more time.

※ ※ ※

Thankfully, Mr. Marvin's outside on the porch, basking in the warm August sunshine. I climb the stairs, take my old seat, and glance over at him. Looks to me like he's gotten even thinner and paler.

He smiles.

I smile back.

We rock.

And rock.

"Hey," he says after a while. "Been making new friends, eh?"

"Yes, at drama camp." After what Leo said, I'm relieved that he said something. I want to keep him interested, so I add, "I've got big news—my Baba's engaged. It's okay, I like her. She's—"

But he interrupts me. "That's good. I'm happy for them. Glad to have one piece of good news to think about. Did you know Leo's mother is about to quit?"

Oh. So he *has* heard the bad news. "If the town builds rentals across the street from us, she and Mr. Corpuz might reconsider and wait for one of those."

Mr. Marvin's gray caterpillar eyebrows climb up his forehead. "Really? I didn't know that was an option."

I frown at the dead roses and rock a bit harder. "I tried to share what was happening on the property, but you didn't want to listen."

"Well . . . you've got a point. I was figuring ignorance

was bliss, but maybe I was wrong. Listen, kid. I've been wanting to tell you: I'm sorry you couldn't convince the town to keep the house. I've been feeling badly about how hard I was on you."

I'm quiet. And then: "It's okay. Actually, you were right. All that work *did* turn out to be a waste of time."

"Well, you gave it a shot. Did you ever finish writing that piece about the woman who owned it?"

So now he's interested? "Sort of, but it didn't matter. I wasn't able to read it aloud at the meeting. I tried, but I did a terrible job. I feel like I let Aunty Lydia down."

Mr. Marvin stops rocking. I look over at him; he's as still and white and small as a bone. "*Aunty* Lydia?" he asks, and his voice sounds strange. "Who's that?"

"Oh, that's what I call Lydia Johnson, the woman who owned the property. I learned about her by reading stuff in boxes that were thrown away. I even found four letters she wrote to her husband."

"Wait . . . you found four PERSONAL LETTERS from LYDIA JOHNSON?!?"

Why is he suddenly so loud? "Yes, Mr. Marvin. But I didn't open them."

"You *sure* you didn't read them?" he asks.

"No, why should I? You know how I feel about privacy. You feel the same way. Besides, Aunty Lydia is one of my heroes. I would never betray her. Those letters belong to her family, if any of them are still alive."

There's a long silence. Then: "One of them is," he says, and his voice sounds strange.

"WHAT? Where? Who?"

Mr. Marvin takes a big breath. "Well, kid, that . . . used to be my family's house, and . . . Lydia Johnson was my mother."

My lower jaw goes slack. "You're . . . *Aunty Lydia's son?*"

"She named me in the Swedish way, in honor of my father. Marvin, son of Anders. Marvin Anderson."

"Mr. Marvin! I can't believe you didn't tell me!"

"I probably should have. Sometimes being too private can be a bad thing."

I'm trying to process this news. "Then those letters belong to you! I'll go get them right now!"

"No need, no need, you can bring them later, but I can't believe those idiot assistants of mine didn't find them first. I showed them the stack of yellow envelopes Mamma wrote to Papa every year on his birthday and told them I was missing four. They were supposed to look before tossing the boxes and make sure those letters weren't there. There's no competence or integrity left in this world." But then he tips his head slightly. "Present company excepted, apparently."

"Umm . . . thanks," I say.

"Of all the people in the world, I'm glad the letters came to you. But you have to promise not to tell anyone about my identity. I've spent a bunch of money keeping it a secret. I don't want to be wined and dined by developers or badgered by do-gooders. So keep it to yourself, will you?"

"I promise I won't tell . . ." And that's when I remember I'm *furious* at Aunty Lydia's descendants!

Mr. Marvin's gazing off into the distance. "Been a long time since I heard someone call her 'Aunty.' That's what the Ichiuji boys called her. The Martinez and Sanchez kids used to call her 'Tía Lydia.'"

I interrupt his reverie. "How could you destroy that place when your mother loved it so much? Why didn't you help us preserve it?"

He shakes his head. "I held on to it for a long time. Even moved back to try and fix up the house and take care of the orchard. But then I fell, broke my hip, and had to move into this place. I hated the thought of selling it, but I had to. Got no family or kin left."

His face is so sad that my anger disappears. "You have me, Mr. Marvin."

"I know, but my life isn't your job. You're a friend, and a kid. You should be enjoying yourself." He sighs. "Now that I've made my decision to sell the place, I can't wait to get it behind me. It's not that I need the money, mind you; I don't have much to spend it on apart from paying for my long-term care here. It's change that's so hard. Take Alodia having to leave this joint to move to

Stockton, of all places. I've been real down about that these last couple of weeks."

Wait a second—Mr. Marvin is the *owner*! He can do whatever he wants with the place! He could even decide to sell the land to the nonprofit! I open my mouth to tell him what to do, but close it again before any words come out. Somehow, the timing feels wrong. Plus, I know how much he hates being bossed around. "I hate change, too," I say instead. "How'd you end up in Minnesota, anyway?"

"After I graduated high school, Mamma sent me to college there. I lived with my grandparents."

"Did she join you?"

"Not until she was much older. She loved the farm and orchard too much. Once she got too frail to live on her own, I brought her back to Minnesota and took care of her there. That's where she's buried, near her parents."

"That reminds me. I . . . I put some flowers on your father's grave. On the first day of the demolition."

"You did? That's sweet. I haven't been able to get over to the cemetery since I fell."

"I loved that orchard and house so much," I say.

"I know. But I still don't get why."

"Well . . . if I keep your secret, will you keep mine?"

He nods. "Sure. That's what friends do."

Friends. Hearing him use that word gives me confidence to confess. I tell him how Ma and I used to sneak into the property to sing and talk, and how I'd go there afterward to write to her. Mr. Marvin reaches over and squeezes my hand. This is a first. He's never done that before.

"My mother used to sing to me on that swing," he says. "I'm glad you and your mother did, too. Gets me kind of choked up to think of it."

He lets go of my hand, pulls a handkerchief out of his pocket, and blows his nose.

"The place *was* falling apart," I say, trying to comfort both of us.

"It was a wreck," Mr. Marvin says. "But still."

"I know."

Silence again.

"I'll bring you her letters," I say after a while.

"Thanks, kid. I'll let you read them after I do."

"You will? I'd love to. Your mother was an amazing person, Mr. Marvin."

"Indeed. Strangely, even though you're Indian and a kid at that, something about you has always reminded me of her. That's why I gave you her hat."

I smile and stand up. "That's one of the best compliments I've heard. Thank you." And then, choosing my words carefully, I leave him with this: "It's up to you to decide what happens next with your beautiful mother's land. But no matter what, Mr. Marvin, you're not getting rid of me again. We're friends for life, you and me."

# FORTY-SIX

THE DAY OF THE DEADLINE for offers arrives. When Baba, Indy, and I are halfway through dinner, Shar bursts into the house. A huge smile is splitting her face in two as she takes her seat. It reminds me of . . . a crack on an apple pie crust . . . no . . . a tear across a sealed envelope. Yes, that's better.

"I've got amazing news!" she says.

"What—that you're going to be on time for dinner one day?" Indy asks, passing her the tureen of lukewarm lentil soup.

"No! Today the real estate agent representing the seller told us the Johnson Family Trust intends to accept the bid from US! From Golden State Dwellings!" And then her voice gets a little choked up. "We got the property. Can you believe it?"

"You've worked so hard," Baba tells her. "I'm so proud of you!"

*I'm* so proud of Mr. Marvin! I'm sure Aunty Lydia

would be proud, too. I gave him her unopened letters; maybe reading them helped him make up his mind.

"How'd you guys manage to elbow out the developers?" Indy asks.

"No idea. We managed to scrape together market price, which was already a lot of money; all the other bidders offered more. But if the sellers want to take our lower bid, that's up to them."

"Any idea who the sellers are?" I ask, keeping my tone light. Drama camp, apparently, has turned me into an Oscar contender.

"Nope. They want to stay anonymous. They had only one request: We have to preserve as many apricot trees as possible, plant a few more, and include a public park with several benches."

"That means you'll still be able to go over there to write, Pandu," Baba says, smiling at me. "Legally, this time."

I smile back. Looks like I might be the only one who knows the truth about the seller, then, and I'm not going to tell a soul. I won't even say anything to him, in fact. He definitely doesn't like a fuss. Don't worry, Mr. Marvin. Pandita Paul was the right confidant.

I jump up. "Okay if I tell Leo?"

"Absolutely," Shar says. "If the Council approves the zoning change, we'll start taking applications right away. The Corpuz family can be first on the list."

"That's a big 'if,'" Baba says, echoing Leo's father. "But so was this, right? Let's host a party to celebrate!"

I race to the phone.

At the party, Leo and I manage the music, switching records on the record player like disc jockeys, and everyone dances to Irene Cara's "Fame" and "Stomp!" by the Brothers Johnson. Even Mr. Flemming loosens his tie and starts dancing the bump with Ms. Consuela.

After this victory, the atmosphere in our house during Golden State Dwellings' meetings is electric. We now have one more roadblock to overcome: convincing the Council to change the zoning in our neighborhood. The vote is scheduled for the first Saturday in September.

As the last days of August speed by, half the town is enraged that the land has been sold to a nonprofit for rental properties. "We're going to block your stupid zoning change," an angry woman shouts at Shar and me outside the grocery store. Her face is tangled with hate, but Shar doesn't flinch and neither do I.

Mr. Marvin brings me up to date on the Ichiuji family's descendants, and he's even called Mr. Ichiuji's grandson to invite him to the Council meeting. We haven't heard back from him yet, but Mr. Marvin's hopeful.

"I'll try and get there, too," he tells me. "Maybe

Alodia can wheel me over. I haven't been out of this prison in a while. Wanted to see that musical of yours, but I wasn't feeling too well that week. Feeling better now, though. Reading those four missing letters from my mother was such a gift. Thanks to you, kid."

"Thanks to *you*, Mr. Marvin," is all I say, figuring we both know what I'm talking about.

He hands back the four yellow envelopes I found, opened now after all these years, along with a whole stack of others. "Here. I think you'll enjoy reading these almost as much as I did."

I read and then reread Aunty Lydia's letters in my room. With each thin, crinkly piece of paper, the handwriting is easier to decipher and she feels closer, nearer, dearer, more alive. I can almost see her holding a chubby baby on her hip—a little Mr. Marvin, who she calls "Podgie," short for "Pojke," which means "boy" in Swedish. What astounds me is the way she signed the letters to Uncle Anders. *Forever, your Lydia*. So close to the way Ma signed her letters to me, and how I signed my letters to her.

After I've read them all through for a second time, I open my desk drawer and pull out the yellow paper that I stashed there weeks ago. I remember for a moment how I tried to share my description of Mr. Marvin's mother at that horrible meeting. And then, spreading out fresh paper on my desk, I start rewriting the story of Aunty Lydia's life. The revised version flows easily now, straight from my heart through the pencil onto the page, almost as if it's poetry, not prose. When I'm done, I change a word here and there, roll the paper up, and secure it with a rubber band. The Council votes tomorrow on the Johnson property. Aunty Lydia should be there.

# FORTY-SEVEN

WE SHOW UP FOR THE zoning meeting early, but the place is already almost full. People keep pouring in. The commercial developers and their supporters are taking seats on the left side of the room, the "keep Sunny Creek as it is" people are on the far right, and rental property advocates have taken over the middle. As Shar, Indy, and I find seats in a row toward the back, Baba and Shef Aunty—that's what she's asked us to call her—walk over to join us.

I'm wearing Aunty Lydia's straw hat to bolster my courage. Now that I know it was hers, I'm going to keep it forever. And wear it, too. I put down the roll of paper on my seat and stay standing for a minute, straightening the pink-and-white shalwar chameez Shef Aunty altered for me.

"Fits perfectly," she says. "Told you I was a good seamstress, didn't I, Anand?"

Baba winks at me. "You did indeed."

The hat doesn't match the shalwar, but who cares? It's a good blend of old and new. We drape jackets and sweaters over five empty places in the row behind us: three for Leo and his parents, two for Jemma and her mother. I use the scarf of the shalwar to stake out a seat on the aisle for Mr. Ichiuji. There's room for Mr. Marvin's wheelchair next to that spot.

Ms. Maryann is near the front, in the middle of the room, of course, near Ms. Margaret, Ms. Harper, Mr. Jackson, and a few other teachers. Señor Alvarez is there, too. He waves and I wave back. Jemma and her mom greet us and take their seats behind us. So do Leo and his father.

Even though Mr. Reed's buddy-buddy with the office developers on the other side of the room, Katrina and her mom, both looking even more blond and tan after their Hawaii vacation, are with her grandmother in the no-change, big-houses crowd. I recognize a few others over there. A couple of teachers, ones who already live here. The vice principal of our school. And one member of the Historical Society, too—Ms. Carol.

Shef Aunty fends off people who try to take the empty seats behind us. Mayor Walsh, Mr. Reed, Councilmember Mathews, and the two other councilmembers file in and take their seats in the semicircle of chairs behind the raised table. I check the back of the room. No sign of Mr. Marvin or Nurse Corpuz. Where are they?

The mayor leads us in the Pledge of Allegiance and the meeting begins.

"Proposed: Sunny Creek Town Council shall change the zoning of the Strawberry Street neighborhood from single-family to multi-family. We shall approve the plan submitted by Golden State Dwellings to build forty rental units on the land recently offered to them by the Johnson Family Trust."

Mayor Walsh looks around the room. "This is a controversial issue, but we welcome civil discussion. Please approach the microphones if you want to speak to this proposal. Line up, please. Slow down, please. No pushing. Let's be civil, neighbors."

Dozens of people are already lining up at the microphones. Two Sunny Creek police officers help them form lines on either side of the room. One by one, townspeople step up to air their opinions.

"Too much traffic with rentals."

"We need affordable housing for our cops."

"Retail and new offices create jobs and bring in tax revenue."

"I want a mix of different kinds of people in my hometown."

"Our schools will get overcrowded if too many new people move to Sunny Creek."

"Teachers shouldn't have to commute two hours to get here."

"That part of town will lose its semirural feel."

And so on. After a while, it starts to sound repetitive.

Even boring. We've heard all these arguments nonstop for weeks now. I shift restlessly in my seat. Is Mr. Marvin okay? Is he coming? Suddenly, there's a commotion in the back of the room. A "no change" opponent of rental properties stops mid-sentence at the microphone. She has a whiny, nasal voice, so I figure everyone must be as relieved as me.

"Excuse us, please." That's Nurse Corpuz!

"Get out of her way, you numbskull!" Mr. Marvin in the house.

I wave wildly to catch Nurse Corpuz's eye. As she wheels my friend through the throng toward the row behind us, they're followed by a Japanese man who's probably Mr. Ichiuji's grandson. Yes, he's taking the seat on the aisle, next to Mr. Marvin's wheelchair.

The person at the microphone clears her throat and restarts her whine. "As I was saying before the interruption . . . Sunny Creek has been a safe town for decades. We don't want low-income rentals luring undesirables into our town and increasing crime. I certainly hope the Council rejects this zoning change proposal."

Undesirables?!!

She's talking about the Corpuz family!

What would Pandita Ramabai do?

What would Aunty Lydia do?

What would *Pandita Paul* do?

I yank the rubber band off the yellow paper and

stand up. Pushing past my family, I stop in the aisle for a second and put my hand on Mr. Marvin's shoulder. "I'm glad you're here. And you, too, Mr. Ichiuji."

The stranger looks confused that I know his name, but he nods a greeting. Mr. Marvin doesn't introduce us. "Go get 'em, kid," he says gruffly. "Nice hat, by the way."

It's Ms. Maryann's turn next for the microphone on our side of the room. The line behind her is long, and I don't want to wait. As I approach her, the librarian glances warily at the yellow paper in my hand, but I don't try and give it to her. Instead, I say, "I want to speak, please."

She gives up her spot without a word.

The whining woman's speech finally comes to a close.

It's my turn.

I'm holding the story that I've revised so carefully, but I don't read it. Instead, I picture eyes of pride and love watching me from an empty seat in the front row. Throwing back my shoulders, I take off Aunty Lydia's hat so my face is in full view, step forward, and start talking.

"Hello, neighbors. I'm here to tell you a story about the family who used to own the property across the street from us. I'm going to call Mr. and Mrs. Johnson 'Uncle Anders' and 'Aunty Lydia' if that's okay with you."

Thanks to the microphone, my voice is loud. But thanks to drama camp, it's clear and resonant. Finally—Pandita Paul has stage presence!

"Even though they died before I was born, I've come

to think of them as a living part of our town. My mother taught me to call adults that I trust 'uncle' and 'aunty,' like kids do in India." I stop and look around at the faces of people who've been fighting one another over the past few weeks. "If we did that here in Sunny Creek, maybe we'd feel closer to each other, like people in Bakkhali, the village where my mother grew up."

"Feel free to call me 'Aunty Bev,' Pandita!" It's Councilmember Mathews, and that gets a laugh.

I smile at her. And then I keep going, telling the story of valiant Aunty Lydia and how she chose to love her neighbors as herself. There's not another sound in the room. Everyone's tuning in; I know a listening silence when I hear it. I catch sight of Shef Aunty's double thumbs-up, Ms. Harper's face, glowing with delight, and Mr. Marvin's intent expression.

I get to the history of the "Keep California White" movement. When I talk about the Japanese families in our valley, I tell the Ichiujis' story and ask their grandson to stand. He takes a small bow and waves at the audience. I wait while they applaud. After the room quiets down, I share about the death of Uncle Anders, the possibility of arson, the birth of their son, Aunty Lydia's upgrading of the Martinez and Sanchez cottages on her property, and how she and the Ichiuji family helped them buy their first houses in the Valley—stories that have become even more clear after reading the letters Mr. Marvin loaned me.

I speak slowly and clearly, taking time to choose the right words to paint a picture of the courageous woman I've come to admire. I'm projecting and enunciating, just as Ms. Harper taught, as I look to the center, the right, and the left. The mayor is listening, the audience murmurs and laughs at the right places, and it looks like even Mr. Reed is paying attention.

"Change is hard; I don't like it much myself. But time moves us forward, no matter how much we hate losing things from the past. And while she loved living near a quiet apricot orchard, I'm sure that my mother, if she were still alive, would welcome forty new neighbors across the street."

I'm coming to a close, so I make eye contact with faces on either side of the aisle: Ms. Maryann, Leo, Jemma, my family, Ms. Margaret, Katrina, and especially those who don't want the zoning to pass. "In a letter to her husband, Lydia Johnson once described heaven as a 'glorious mix of many different kinds of people dwelling together in peace and joy.' She wrote this, too: 'My mission is to make Sunny Creek a bit more like heaven.' Well, that's our mission, too, especially here, in 'the Valley of Heart's Delight,' as Silicon Valley used to be called." I turn to face the Council. "I hope you agree."

When I stop, there's applause, and not just from the middle of the room. I smile again, but I can feel the stage presence departing. Putting Aunty Lydia's hat back on,

I start making my way back to my family, but people along the aisles stop me to shake my hand.

"Wonderful!"

"Powerful!"

"You really turned the tide, kid!"

"Great job!"

Sliding into my chair, I lean into Indy, who puts her arm around me. A few more people take the microphone, but the fighting spirit in the room seems to have evaporated. Even opponents to the plan sound nicer than they did before I shared about Aunty Lydia. The line gets shorter and shorter until there's nobody left who wants to speak.

Mayor Walsh calls for a vote.

It's still tight, three to two, but the zoning change is approved. The mayor must have voted for us. There's even a slim chance that Mr. Reed did, too. Katrina had written on a postcard from Hawaii that she was working hard to change his mind.

"This meeting is adjourned," the mayor says. "Let's leave without any trouble, neighbors, in honor of Lydia Johnson. Aunty Lydia, I mean."

And her son, too, I think, but Podgie's secret is safe with me.

# FORTY-EIGHT

ON THE LAST DAY OF summer vacation, I'm home alone reading *The Secret Garden*. A delivery truck pulls up outside our house, and two burly men jump out.

I put down my book and head outside. "Is that something for the Paul family?"

"Yep. For someone named Pan-dee-tah Paul?"

"That's me."

As the two men unload the truck, I can't believe my eyes.

It's the porch swing from the Johnson house!

I'd thought it was gone forever, deep in a landfill or incinerated, but here it is, intact and whole. The delivery guys carry it to our porch and hand me a letter, which I tear open as soon as they're gone.

*Dear Pandita, I had my assistants rescue and restore the swing before the demolition because it reminded me so much of my mother. I want you to have it. I didn't tell you about it because I like surprises. And secrets. Here's to keeping ours. Affectionately, Mr. Marvin, aka "Podgie."*

Quickly, I unbutton the cover on the cushion that's on the left side of the seat. I can't believe it.

My precious, precious letters from Ma are still inside!

And all the letters I wrote to her, just as I left them. Plus the one blank notecard and envelope I left behind in June.

Oh, thank God, Ma's girlhood photo, too!

I drop a kiss on it, just like I always used to, and give it five more.

After putting the blank notecard on the cushion next to me, I jump up to store my precious possessions in my room and grab a pen. When I get back, I notice that Aunty Lydia's swing is blocking the front door so it can't open all the way. And our family clutter is jammed around it. Maybe it's time to clean this porch up. After lugging the broken chairs, skateboard, and tricycle to the side of the house by the trash cans, I sweep the porch and dust off the swing. Then I haul around a few more rattan chairs and a table from the backyard.

There.

Now our porch looks inviting.

I'll figure out what to say and what not to say when Baba and my sisters ask about the swing. Choosing the right words is my knack, as Mr. Marvin says.

Exhaling, I sink into my familiar seat and take stock of the Johnson property across the street. In October, crews will start building the first of what Golden State Dwellings is calling the "Lydia Johnson Townhouses." The Corpuz family's application was one of the first to be accepted, and Leo's father agreed to wait out the construction in their Sunny Creek apartment. I can hardly wait until school starts next week, especially now that Leo's sticking around. But it's not just spending time with him, it's being with Jemma, Katrina, and the other kids I got to know better during drama camp.

Me, Pandita Paul, counting down the days until eighth grade?

Now *there's* a plot twist.

Maybe you don't need just one best friend. Maybe it's better to have a mix, just as Aunty Lydia said. Old, young, rich, poor, new to town, people with deep roots, even loved ones from the past.

I pick up the pen and the lavender notecard. From the branches of an apricot tree still standing across the street comes the birdsong that reminds me of Ma's voice. I date my letter September 7th, 1980. It feels like she already knows everything I'm about to tell her. But that's okay. By now I know that these letters are for me. I start writing anyway.

*My darling Ma, I have so, so much to share with you . . .*

# THE FOUR MISSING LETTERS OF
# LYDIA JOHNSON

18th of May, 1906. My dearest husband. Today is your twenty-fifth birthday, and you've been gone a month now. I still can hardly believe it. I hated hearing certain people share memories of you at the funeral—people who condemned us for standing up for our neighbors, now acting like friends, calling you a hero. I didn't cry in front of them. Later, though, when the Ichiuji family came with a basket of food and fresh flowers, I did cry. Oh, Anders! Seeing their cow come out of the barn, safe and untethered, just before the roof collapsed with you inside. Yutaka and her sister holding me back. How I replay that terrible moment in my head, over and over.

"How can we ever repay you?" Paul Ichiuji keeps asking. He and Yutaka bring gifts and food; they feel so guilty that you died trying to save their animals and their barn.

Why did the brigade take so long to come to their farm? They put out other fires that started in the area after the quake, but they didn't show up for the Ichiujis until much later. I fear it's because of growing hatred against the Japanese. There's talk throughout the state of changing the law so that people born in Japan can no longer own property and land. If such an unjust law passes, Paul's ready to transfer the title of his property to one of his twins, but they're only two years old!

It's shameful, this "Keep California White" campaign. We'll probably never know who caused the delay in sending the brigade, but the Maker sees all, and if there was nefarious intent, that will be punished one day. This I believe. And that I'll be with you in eternity, Anders, as Pastor reminds me. I've always thought of heaven as a glorious mix of different kinds of people who dwell together in peace and joy. Well, my mission is to make Sunny Creek a bit more like heaven until I see you again.

It seems like yesterday that my cousin and I came for a visit to San Francisco and, on a whim, attended that church social. What if we hadn't? I noticed you right away, and soon you walked over to me, carrying that big slice of caramel almond cake. "It's called toscakaka in Sweden, where I was born," you told me. "One day my mother will teach you how to make it." So bold—on the first day we met! I think I fell in love with you at that moment. Oh, how my parents raged when I told them I was marrying you! And now, a year after we eloped, our child grows bigger every day. I can still feel the warmth of your hands measuring my waist. I remember how you dropped kisses there, and told my stomach stories your Mormor told you, even though we laughed at the thought of a baby listening.

Now who will speak to this child in Swedish? I'm too American, I won't be able to pronounce the words like you would have. But I'll try to learn a few. For your sake, I'll try. And if it's a boy, I'll name him Marvin Anderson, and we'll call him by the nickname they gave you as a child—"'Podgie,' short for 'Pojke,' which means 'boy,'" as you told me. I'll work in the orchard with him, slinging him on my back in that kripp-sack that belonged to your mother.

Life presses me on. There are apricot saplings to tend, a baby soon to care for, and a newly built house to furnish. Nothing to sit on but the chairs and table you built. And this porch swing. Oh, how I love it! Remember the fun we had buying it on our outing to San Francisco? What an extravagance, Anders! But you insisted because I wanted it so.

I'm sitting here now, remembering Sunday afternoons when we watched the sunlight fall across our land and trees. No wonder they call this area the Valley of Heart's Delight. The trees and hills and flowers around here make it feel like the Garden of Eden. But what is Eden without you, my darling? A desert. A Valley of Dry Bones. How I long to hold and see you again! I love you, Anders. From now until I join you in eternity, I pledge to write a letter to you every year on your birthday. The baby comes soon. Pray for us. Forever, your Lydia.

(2)

18th of May, 1924. My dearest Anders, happiest of birthdays. The trees are in bloom, and thanks to kind help, our farm is thriving. This year we were able to build comfortable cottages for the Martinez and Sanchez families. We continue to share the profits from the harvest with them, and in turn, they have been so good to us.

My parents wrote and told me—no, ordered me—to sell the orchard and move back to Minnesota now that Podgie's enrolled in college close to them. A woman shouldn't be farming alone, they say, especially with "foreigners living on the property and next door." Foreigners? The Martinez and Sanchez families feel closer than my blood relatives. As do the Ichiujis. Their sons Fred and Sam are now in their third year of college, and thankfully for their parents, they're studying nearby. I'm counting down the days until Podgie comes home for the summer. I suspect my parents offered to pay for his college education so he would settle near them, and their plan might be working.

In ten days, the United States government is going to vote on a terrible law, Anders. If it passes, it will completely ban immigration from Asia. I've heard President Coolidge supports this atrocious proposal, and many other elected officials are talking about how America must stay American. What they mean, of course, is white. This disgraceful practice of excluding Asians is growing like a cancer in this country. The worst part is that my own parents are part of it. I only hope they won't try to poison Podgie with their narrow views. His heart will be steadfast, I'm sure of it. He is your son through and through. Seventeen years old and doing so well in college! I write often to your parents about him. Sweden suffered food shortages during the terrible war, but Podgie and I sent money regularly, and they survived it.

Meanwhile, my parents say all will be forgiven if I come back. As if THEY need to forgive ME, Anders! They made their choice by cutting us out of their lives. All that ranting about you not being educated and from another country. So what if I was born in the U.S.A. but you weren't? Your craft in wood, your skill with farming and fruit . . . they could neither see those talents nor treasure them like I did. It's been seventeen years, and my heart still longs for you. Forever, your Lydia.

18th of May, 1942. My dear Anders. Happiest of Birthdays, beloved husband. Once again, this country is at war. After the bombing of Pearl Harbor last December, the existing suspicion and hatred of our dear Japanese neighbors exploded throughout this Valley. President Roosevelt signed an executive order in February that requires Japanese people living in Western states to move inland to internment camps. All people with Japanese ancestry, even if they were born in the United States like Fred and Sam, are being sent by bus to one of those prisons in Arizona. After paying taxes and being a part of this community for so many years! With two of the Ichiuji grandsons enlisted in the U.S. Army, fighting for the country they love! This is truly an evil time. We're fighting the Nazis but I hope we're not becoming like them at the same time.

When I waved goodbye to Paul and Yutaka and their families, Yutaka and I were weeping. I promised that we would protect their property while they are imprisoned by our government. Scoundrels without scruples are already eyeing the land and equipment owned by departing Japanese farmers. Somehow, Luis, Rafael, their children, Podgie, and I will irrigate and tend and harvest the Ichiujis' fifteen acres of strawberries along with our orchard. We also plan to stand guard at night so that nobody can steal this dear family's equipment. The Valley of Heart's Delight is not a good name for this place. Hatred continues to burn in the hearts of people.

Still, our trees bloom and bring forth fruit. I'm sitting in our porch swing overlooking them now, taking in big breaths of their fragrance. My heart aches at times, missing Podgie so much, but when I sit here with you, I'm never lonely. Forever, your Lydia.

(4)

18th of May, 1956. My beloved Anders, happiest of birthdays. Thanks to the Martinez and Sanchez families, our orchard is surviving. We are even turning a profit. So much so, Luis and Maria were able to put a down payment on a house in East Meadow. They are moving shortly, and while I am so happy for them, I'm not sure what I'll do without them living on the property. But, oh, I wish them well. Now for the Sanchez family to find a home! Of course then I'll truly be alone on the farm.

All around us, neighbors are selling orchards right and left and new ranch houses are being built. The Ichiuji boys sold their strawberry farm last summer. They got a good price for it, but I was sad to lose them as neighbors. Paul and Yutaka have settled in Pacific Grove to live near Sam and his family. I'm thinking of visiting them soon.

I miss Podgie so much, Anders. I wish he could visit more often, but he's busy running Father's company. He keeps asking me to move to Minnesota. "You're getting older, Mother," he says, and he's right. But what to do with the farm? Our apricot trees bring me joy. They connect me to you, Anders. I'll get up in a minute to cut some sprigs for inside, so the blossoms can fill our home with their fragrance. I'll never tire of our orchard. Or this porch swing of ours, where I'll write to you every year until I see you again one day. Soon, and very soon. Forever, your Lydia.